STAND FAST

EARLY WARNING SERIES #3

ANGUS MCLEAN

Published 2020 by Smoking Gun Publications

ISBN 978 0 473 56091 1

ALSO BY ANGUS MCLEAN

Chase Investigations Series

Old Friends

Honey Trap

Sleeping Dogs

Tangled Webs

Dirty Deeds

Red Mist

Fallen Angel

Holy Orders

Deal Breaker

The Division Series

Smoke and Mirrors

Call to Arms

The Shadow Dancers

The Berlin Conspiracy

No Second Chance

Nicki Cooper Mystery Series

The Country Club Caper

Early Warning Series

Martial Law

Getting Home

Stand Fast

STAND FAST

BY ANGUS MCLEAN

1

It had been four days since things turned to shit, and a lot had changed.

Instead of just our family of three living the quiet life on our small property in rural North Waikato, we also now had three grandparents and a work colleague living with us. We were surrounded by people who were poorly prepared for such an event. Thieves and thugs were roaming the countryside, taking what they could get and killing indiscriminately. Martial law had been imposed and the military were deployed to the streets.

It had been four days since I'd seen my wife, Gemma, until she and her workmate Alex turned up home in a hail of bullets, pursued by a family of psychos they had crossed paths with. That had been yet another gunfight, this time practically on our doorstep. I'd lost count of how many people I'd killed in the last four days. How many my father-in-law Rob had killed. Christ, even my own mother, Jenny, had gunned down a lowlife who had shot at my son and tried to rob our place.

Even in years as a street cop, I'd never seen carnage like this, especially not in such a short space of time. People had gone mad. Ever since a giant earthquake, probably the biggest the country had ever seen, had knocked out Wellington and forced the Prime Minister to declare a national state of emergency, people had just lost their shit.

My family was prepared for a natural disaster, but even we were not fully ready for what hit us. Most people were caught completely unawares, and it showed.

As the early morning sunlight broke through a crack in the curtains, I watched Gemma sleeping. She'd been on the road with Alex the last four days, walking from central Auckland to get home. She'd told me some of the story last night as we sat in the darkness, sipping whiskey and regrouping.

She had talked and cried as she finally started to process it all, and to let go of the stress she'd been under. Alex had chipped in as well, and his respect for her was obvious. He told us numerous times that he wouldn't have made it without her.

They'd dodged crooks, been forced to kill on multiple occasions to defend themselves, and braved the elements and the people they'd come across. It had been a hell of an adventure, if you could call it that, and certainly nothing she had ever contemplated happening.

Gemma was a normal woman, working part-time in an office, running around after me and our 7-year old son Archie, keeping an eye on her elderly parents. Keeping the wheels turning. But she was tough, tougher than she had ever realised, and it was her mental strength and determination that had ultimately got them home.

It had taken a long time for things to settle down yesterday. Archie was excited to see his Mum again, and her parents, Rob and Sandy, had been incredibly relieved too. Even my own mother, never a great fan of her daughter-in-law, had been glad to see her. Gemma and Alex had both taken the opportunity to have a proper wash with hot water and soap, to wash their hair, brush their teeth and put on clean clothes. I had loaned some clothes to Alex, who only had what he had carried. My clothes were baggy on him but they would do.

Gemma had stayed on Archie's bed until he went to sleep.

Even though we'd been up late I'd been awake since before dawn, as had become my habit. I had quietly patrolled the house and checked outside, but nothing seemed disturbed. Fully clothed, I'd sat back on the bed and watched over Gemma as she slept.

She twitched in her sleep and had woken during the night, reaching out for me, wanting the comfort of knowing I was there. She was battered from her ordeal, physically and emotionally. A graze on her cheek was healing and would soon fade. We had iced her ribs and back where she'd been booted, and anti-inflammatories would help sort that out soon enough.

I sat in the dim grey light, listening to her breathing. Keeping watch.

I couldn't quite believe she was home.

2

The neighbours arrived while we were tidying up after breakfast and getting ready for the day.

Rusty and Sophie from over the road had been over the previous day, relieved to see Gemma home safe and sound. Others had come down after the firefight we'd had right outside our drive-way, some coming armed and ready to assist, albeit too late. It had been a short, violent encounter in which we'd killed all three of the thugs chasing Gemma and Alex, and the road had ended up littered with bullet casings and blood.

Jenny saw the neighbours coming first, gathering on the road outside our place.

'Looks like we've got visitors,' she said, drying dishes as she looked out the kitchen window.

I came through from the dining room, tucking in my T-shirt. There looked to be maybe fifteen of them. I turned to Rob.

'Come for a walk?' I said, and he shrugged.

'Why not.'

'Come on Dad,' Archie said, grabbing his sneakers. 'Let's go see what's going on.'

The three of us headed down the drive together. As had become habit, Rob and I both wore our gunbelts and carried our rifles. He had a 9mm Browning High Power on his hip and a Lee Enfield Mk 4 .303 in his hands. Mine were a Ruger GP100 and a lever action Rossi Puma, both in .357 Magnum. Archie carried a stick he had been throwing for the dog, who also tagged along, his tail wagging happily.

We met the crowd at the end of the drive, all familiar faces. Clyde and Ellette, the left-wing academics from next door. Brenton and Linda from further up, Brenton all recovered from the near-miss he'd had a couple of days ago – it wasn't often you walked away from a 7mm round with barely a scratch. Amy, the woman who we had rescued with her kids and helped to relocate to the Macklin house on our other side. I noticed that Bevan wasn't there – probably still pissed with me.

'Morning everyone,' I said.

'We hear that Gemma made it home,' Linda said without preamble. 'How's she doing?'

'Pretty good,' I said. 'It wasn't easy, but they made it.'

Questions started flying about how things were "out there", what they'd seen, what they could tell us. I sent Archie back to get Gemma and he ran off with Jethro bouncing along at his side. I answered what I could, and when she arrived, Gemma was bombarded with so many questions that it felt like a press conference.

She answered as much as she could and gave them whatever information she could share. It got surprisingly emotional – surprising to me, anyway – as people realised how screwed things actually were.

'It sounds the Walking Dead out there,' Amy said.

'Except it's not zombies,' Gemma said. 'It's everyday people.'

Clyde gave a dismissive *pfftt*. 'It won't be average people,' he said, giving her that superior down-the-nose look that he liked. 'Criminals, sure, and the marginalised people in society, desperate for food. I can understand that.'

'Do people need looted TVs to survive?' Gemma retorted. 'Because that's what they're doing. We saw people getting beaten up, we saw shops getting broken into. We had people trying to rob us, trying to kill us.' She glared hard at him. 'Have you left here since this all happened, Clyde?'

'Well, no, but...'

'So you have no idea,' she told him. She looked to me, and I shrugged.

'You can't legislate for stupid,' I said.

Gemma gave a ghost of a smile and someone laughed. Clyde's face reddened.

'And what about yesterday?' he said, taking another tack. 'Who were those people you brought here?'

It was my turn to glare at him. 'If you mean who were the fuckin' psychos who chased my wife and her friend and tried to kill them, we don't know. They'd been chasing them for a couple of days and these guys couldn't get away. Luckily for us all, Rob and I were able to help out and stop them.'

'You mean kill them?' The down-the-nose look was back.

'Yeah, we killed them.' I stepped forward, angry now, ready to have it out with him. 'They had the option of turning round and getting the hell outta here, but they chose to try and kill two people who were just tryin' to get home. They brought the fight.'

He sneered at me. 'And you finished it.'

'Yeah,' I grated. 'We finished it.'

'Well without knowing the real story behind it all, it's very hard for us to judge,' Clyde said, glancing round at the other neighbours. Nobody else said a thing, not even a nod of agreement.

'Nobody's asking you to judge anything, Clyde,' I said. 'I don't give a fuck if you don't like it. Tell you what, I'll give you a gun and you can deal with any shitheads that come round, shall I? Does that work for you?'

He gave the dismissive *pfftt* again, and he smiled at his wife, who had been listening silently. She looked on the verge of tears which, I'd learned, was her go-to reaction for anything unpleasant.

'I really don't think...'

'That's right,' Gemma cut him off. 'You don't.'

I looked around at the rest of the neighbours. 'The good thing is, from those arseholes yesterday, we recovered some firearms and ammo. If any of you want them, you're welcome to have them.'

There were a few "yeses" and Clyde looked horrified. Ellette gave in to the waterworks and started sobbing.

'You can't be serious?' Clyde said, hugging his wife to his chest. 'You think we need more guns? After everything that's happened?'

'Yep, I do. *Because* of everything that's happened.' I looked round at them all again. 'This isn't going to end in a hurry, people. You need to be prepared to defend yourself and your family, and also your neighbours. Those of you that want a gun, come with me.'

I led a small group of them up the drive, Rob and Gemma following along. Laid out on the garage floor were some of the guns we'd taken yesterday – a SKS 7.62mmx39, a Winchester 12-gauge pump action, a bolt action Ruger 7mm, and a bolt action Norinco .22.

The other weapons we'd taken, the better ones, were tucked away out of sight. Brenton took the shotgun, Amy the Norinco, and the other two went to other neighbours from further up the road. I gave them all the ammo we had for the weapons as well, and we walked together back down the drive. Clyde and Ellette had gone already, so it was easier to talk.

'I'll come round later and show you all how to use these, if you like,' I said.

'I'm okay with this,' one of them said, hefting the SKS. 'I had a few years in the TF.'

It was Darren, a hobby farmer/building engineer. I vaguely knew him; he had a wife and older kids, from memory. It was good to know he had some military experience.

The other guy, Sean, had done some hunting too, so he was all good with the Ruger 7mm bolt action. Brenton and Amy were happy to take some help.

'Other thing is,' I said, 'I'm thinking we should block off the end of the road. It might help prevent baddies coming down here. They see a blockade and people with guns, they're more likely to look for a softer target.'

There were nods and murmurs, so I pushed on with a plan. We

agreed to meet mid-morning and get that organised, and they headed off their separate ways. I watched them go, four ordinary civilians now toting arms and planning to defend their community against the hordes.

Gemma must have read my mind. 'Things have changed,' she said quietly.

I nodded and put my arm around her shoulders. There was no arguing with that – I had the feeling that things had changed forever.

3

The meth and weed smoke wafting from the community hall carried on the light breeze, and Aroha wrinkled her nose in disgust.

She pegged out the last of her washing on the line – hand-washed in cold water – and picked up the basket. She knew what Jake and those boys did. Hell, she'd done her own share of shit back in the day, but these boys were something else. The anger they carried, the violence – it was different. Well past seventy years old now and she'd seen a lot, even did a couple of short stints in the klink as a young woman.

Not these days. These days she got the pension and spent most of it on her garden and putting petrol in her little Nissan, food on the table for her kids that didn't get enough to eat at home.

It saddened her to see how these young ones lived now – it was all Playstations and cars and booze and drugs and fighting and screwing around. She did what she could to set a good example for them, but it was a lone voice. Even though she had stopped Jake from stomping that fool Tintz, the young ones didn't listen like they used to. Didn't have the same respect.

It hadn't saved Tintz anyway, he'd died from his injuries and wouldn't leave a huge hole in the world. Aroha had known his grand-mother and his mother, and wasn't surprised he'd turned out how he had.

She stopped on the back path of her little cottage and felt the sun warm on her face. Autumn now; winter was coming. Her vegetable garden and the chooks she kept would keep her going through the winter, even with no power on, but she worried about her neigh-bours. Most of them didn't have the same skills she had, the ability to make something from nothing, the experience of living through hardship and just making do.

Now with Little Dog and his Bandits in town, things weren't going to improve. All she'd seen was guns and drugs and fighting. One of the young girls down the street had been raped by one of them last night, came home bleeding and crying to her aunty. Nothing they could do about it. Aroha was inclined to deal with it herself, confront the man – she'd done it before, more than once – but not with them all hopped up like they were.

The roar of a motorcycle reached her, the gunning of a throttle and the screeching of tyres. Smoke began rising from the main street and Aroha put her washing basket down, walking round to the front of her house. From her corner property she could see up the main street and also down her little cul-de-sac.

A Bandit on a hog was doing a burnout in front of the community hall, thick grey and black smoke pouring into the air, people cheering and yahooing like fools. Someone threw a bottle and it smashed on the road. Aroha tut-tutted under her breath and wandered up that way, tucking her hands into the pockets of her apron. The apron bore the slogan *World's Greatest Nana* and she wore it with pride.

The burnout had finished by the time she got there and the biker was idling outside the hall, talking and laughing with his buddies.

Aroha walked over to where the broken glass was and bent down, slowly picking the pieces up. She got the biggest piece in her leathery hand and started filling it with the smaller pieces. She heard laughter from over the way but she ignored it and carried on. She hadn't finished before she heard the scuff of boots and a shadow fell over her.

She ignored it and carried on.

'Whaddaya doin'?' a gruff voice said.

Aroha turned her head enough to see the knees of his dirty black jeans. 'Picking up glass,' she said. She carried on, shuffling forward bent over, reaching for another piece.

'Whaddaya doin' that for?'

Aroha sighed. She picked up the last big piece and added it to the pile in her hand. She straightened up, her back stiff, and looked at the man. He was a surprisingly skinny guy, unshaven with gappy teeth. Thirty, maybe. The leather vest he wore had a Prospect badge on it, so she knew he was a wannabe.

'Because,' Aroha said, gathering herself, 'some fool threw a bottle. Kids walk here, and I don't want my *mokapuna* getting cut feet. You understand?'

'Huh.' He grinned and looked back over to his buddies, who were watching from outside the hall. 'Fuck 'em and fuck their feet. Ain't shit to me. An' you callin' me a fool, old lady?'

Aroha eyed him, straightening up to her full height – just level with his shoulder. 'Did you throw the bottle?' she said.

'Eh.' He snorted and spat on the road beside her. She felt some of the warm spittle land on her bare arm.

'Well yes, then I am saying you're a fool.'

The guy's smirk twisted and he glanced at his buddies again, maybe looking for support, maybe showing off. Aroha didn't know, but whatever it was, she knew he was a bad man. But she'd had a lifetime of bad men.

'Eh,' he said, 'I ain't call you names, old lady. Why you call me a fool?'

'Well, son,' Aroha smiled. 'Give me your hand.'

Without waiting, she reached out and took his hand. She carefully placed the broken glass in it and smiled again. He looked at the glass then glared at her.

'Whadda fuck?'

'Now if you put that in the bin, I'll take back my thoughts of you being a fool,' Aroha said. She patted his hand. 'Thank you.'

The guy scowled and threw the glass on the road, smashing it more. 'I ain't your fuckin' nigger boy, old lady,' he snarled. 'You fuckin' talk to me like that...'

He was suddenly propelled sideways, staggering and clutching at the side of his head where Jake had hooked him. Jake was on him, grabbing him by the neck and jerking him forward, snatching his head and rolling it, spinning him off his feet so he crashed to the ground. Before the guy could get up, Jake kicked him in the ribs and stood over him.

'The fuck you think you are, boy?' he growled, fists bunched. The guy cowered beneath him. 'You think you the man here, boy? You talk to my nan like that, I'll rip your fuckin' head off.'

'Sorry Jake, I didn't...'

'Fuck up.' Jake kicked him again. 'Get up, cunt.'

The guy did so, and Jake dropped him with a big uppercut.

'Get up.'

They repeated the process two more times before Aroha stepped forward.

'Jake,' she said. 'Thank you for standing up for me.'

He paused, breathing hard, and looked at her. 'Can't have this shit, Nan.'

'I know,' she said, nodding and touching his arm. 'Thank you. That's enough.'

He looked at her, and she could see the bloodlust in his eyes. 'Sure?'

'Well,' she relented. 'He still needs to pick up the glass he broke.'

'Hear that, motherfucker?' Jake stood over the guy, who was bleeding from the mouth and nose now. 'Pick up that glass, or I'll fuck you up. Eh?'

The guy nodded meekly. 'Sorry Jake.'

Jake turned to Aroha, who nodded and smiled. 'Thank you, Jake,' she said. 'How about you come down to mine and have a nice cuppa?'

Jake smiled, looking like a little boy again. 'Okay, Nan,' he said.

4

Bevan was outside his house when I arrived, and he looked pissed off.

'Morning mate,' I said, as breezily as I could manage. 'Going to barricade the end of the road – you free to help?'

Bevan scowled. 'I'm not having it, Mark,' he said. 'It's bullshit, and you know it.'

I stopped short of him. 'What's the problem?' I said.

I knew full well what his problem was going to be, but he needed to spell it out before I would waste my time. Bevan was a strange little man at the best of times, and I'd had more to do with him in the last few days than I had the whole time we'd lived there. He lived alone and only worked when he felt like it. I'd heard he'd had some kind of compensation claim against a previous employer and won big, allowing him to be mortgage free while still in his early thirties.

He scowled harder. 'You shouldn't've taken those guns,' he said. 'And I saw you giving them away, too. You shouldn't've done that, too.'

'Mate, they don't belong to you,' I said, summonsing my patience from a short supply. 'I think I'm quite entitled to do whatever the hell I want with them. They were used against my family, after all.'

'I helped,' he sulked.

'No, you didn't. Not that time. Besides, don't you have enough guns already?'

'That's not the point, and you know it's not.' His face darkened. 'You think those people you gave them to know how to use them? Are they as good as me?' He hefted his front-slung AR-15 and adopted a pose he probably saw in Soldier of Fortune.

I almost laughed, but you never knew with Bevan. I was pretty sure he had mental health issues of some sort, which didn't mix well with firearms. Unfortunately, the options for a buddy in a tight corner had been slim lately.

'Look, we need people around us that are ready to step up and protect our community,' I said. 'These guys have all put their hands up, and it makes sense to share the love.' I glanced over my shoulder at the small group walking up the road towards us. 'In fact, here they come now. We're going to block the road off; are you helping or not?'

He grunted and scowled.

'Good. How about you drive the Ford ute down and I'll get these guys to push the car?'

Darren, Sean, Brenton, and one of Darren's kids had come down. Alex and Rob were coming along behind them. Between us we got both vehicles down to the intersection at the top of our road, and manhandled the busted up white Honda sedan across the road. It had refused to start since Gemma and Alex got home in it, and was so full of holes as to be next to useless except as a roadblock.

The gap on either side of it was about half a lane or so wide, and we blocked up one side with fallen trees, making it impassable without a bulldozer. The other side was just wide enough for a vehicle, and we had some debate about blocking that off too.

In the end we agreed that it made sense to be able to still get out if we needed to, so that side was filled by the Ford F-150. It still ran fine and could just be driven out of the way.

'What do we do with the key?' Darren asked, wiping sweat from his brow. He was a wide-shouldered guy with a dark beard and a big belly. It was a long time since he'd been a reserve soldier.

'If we have a guard here, they can hold it,' I said. 'Otherwise we either leave it here, or someone holds onto it.'

'Who's going to guard it?' Brenton said. 'I dunno if we could get any of the other neighbours to do that.'

'Not fuckin' Clyde, anyway,' Bevan chipped in. 'He's a fuckin' homo.'

'Really?' Alex put on a camp voice and gave an exaggeratedly-excited grin. 'Oooh, I really must meet him. Clyde, you say?'

Everybody laughed, but Alex wasn't finished yet. He made eyes at Bevan, and I saw the anger in Bevan's face. He stepped forward and gave Alex a hard push in the chest, sending him back a few feet and stopping the laughter dead. He put his hand back on his AR-15 and I stepped in, clapping one hand onto the weapon and the other onto his shoulder.

'Don't be stupid,' I growled. 'He's only having a laugh.'

'He's bein' all gay and shit,' Bevan said, trying to pull the rifle free and scowling at Alex, who had fallen silent. 'You think I'm a fuckin' fag, boy?'

I jerked him off-balance by his shoulder and shook him. 'Calm the fuck down, Bevan,' I said. 'It was just a joke. You pull that weapon and things'll go bad for you, understand?'

He backed down and I let him go. The whole group had gone silent and the collaborative mood had disappeared. Darren and his boy made their excuses and hurried off, Sean and Brenton hard on their heels.

Bevan muttered something under his breath, spat and stalked off towards his house. Rob and I looked at each other. The older man shook his head and sucked his teeth.

'The guy's nuts,' he said. 'He's going to be a problem for us, I tell you that now.'

'I think you're right,' I said. 'Sorry Alex, I've never seen him act out like that before.'

He shrugged. 'I've put up with that sort of shit for years,' he said. 'Homophobia's all the rage in provincial New Zealand.'

I paused for a moment before realisation hit me.

'Oh,' I said. 'Oh, right...gotcha.'

Rob was still confused, looking from me to Alex.

'I'm gay,' Alex said, and Rob laughed out loud.

'Wow,' he said. 'That explains that, then.'

'And Bevan?' I asked, already having my own suspicions from his reaction.

Alex shrugged again. 'He's in denial,' he said.

Rob laughed again and I cocked an eyebrow at Alex.

'Violently so,' I said, and he nodded.

'Yep,' he said. 'I didn't quite click until that moment, but I'd say he's got some issues. And now he hates me.'

'You think so?'

'Oh, I know so. He knows that I know, and because he's in denial, and because he's just embarrassed himself in front of all of you, he's not a happy bunny at all.'

'Great,' I said. 'That's all we need.'

5

F ood was getting tight but Aroha still had some homemade chocolate chip cookies left.

She put two on a plate and served them to Jake at the table while the pot boiled. With the electricity out she had reverted to using a gas ring on the benchtop, the LPG cylinder sitting in the corner of the bench. She still had plenty of tea yet, but shared a bag between the two mugs anyway, as she always had. It paid to be frugal, now more than ever.

She added sugar to both cups, no milk, and sat with him at the table.

'Thanks Nan.' Jake smiled and took his drink.

Aroha pushed the plate towards him. 'Help yourself, son. I know you like my homemade things best.'

Jake nodded and took one. She had always been the best baker in town.

They were silent for a few moments while they sipped their black tea and Jake finished off the first cookie and went on to the second one. Aroha broke the silence.

'When'd you last eat, Jake?'

He shrugged and munched. 'Dunno. While ago.'

'You been on that funny stuff?'

He frowned and washed down his mouthful of cookie. 'I like a bit,' he said.

Aroha frowned too. 'I don't like that stuff. Makes people do things. You should stick to the herb, Jake. Herb never made people violent like that other stuff, that P.'

Jake worked his tongue to get a piece of cookie from behind a tooth. Every last bit was worth having, in his opinion.

'I do that too,' he grinned.

'You know what I mean, Jake. I never say nothing to you about what you do, eh? All the things that happen over the years, I never growl or say nothing, do I?'

'True.'

Aroha took a sip of her tea. It was still scalding hot and she decided to leave it a while. She noticed that her heart was off at a gallop and she took a breath to get things under control. No need to be so anxious talking to Jake; she'd known him since he was a boy.

'Things goin' a bit crazy round here just now, eh?'

Jake nodded again and folded his hands together, elbows on the table while he waited for her to get to the point.

'I don't like all the violence,' Aroha finally said. She could still give a good stern look, and she fixed him with one now. 'I don't like all these boys bein' around here, in our town. Causin' trouble.'

'They ain't causin' trouble, Nan,' Jake said, and her stern look got sterner.

'They out there drinkin' and fightin' and drivin' like fools on their bikes,' she said. 'And the girl, Minnie? What happened there ain't right.'

Jake set his jaw. 'That girl come to one o' the boys, got what she come for and din't like it after. That's all that is, ain't no rape and shit like she says.'

'She's only fourteen, Jake,' Aroha insisted. 'It ain't even legal.'

Jake snorted. 'An' what's legal now, Nan? Never stopped no one anyways.'

Aroha's heart was damn near bruising her ribs from the inside.

This wasn't going like it should. 'Your friend, the one in the big fancy car?'

'Aye.'

'I don't like him. He'll get you in trouble, Jake. You need to stay away from him, son.'

Jake scowled now, and she knew the conversation was over. 'That bullshit ain't happenin', Nan. I'll forget you said that...this time. All I hear from you today is "I don't like". Won't be sayin' that when we bring food and shit back to town, will you? New table for you? New TV? You don't want none o' that?'

'I don't need none o' that, Jake.' She reached across the table and touched his hand. 'I need you safe, that's what I need.'

Jake scowled some more and hissed through his teeth. 'This is it, Nan. This is what I do. Gangster for life, eh.' He sat back and clapped his fist to his chest, eyeballing her. 'Done the time, done it hard, took everything they could throw at me.' He cocked his head back and looked at her, his eyes dark pools. 'Ain't never gunna break me, tell you that now. Bandits always there for me, an' now I'm back with them. Only way a nigger like me ever gunna get ahead is with my brothers.'

Aroha shook her head sadly, saying nothing. She had seen many like him come and go, and she had never given up hoping. Jake's nostrils flared when he read the look on her face.

'This ain't your thing, Nan,' he said. 'You done your time way back when, you run with the brothers back then eh. That was your time.'

'Bad times,' Aroha said softly.

Jake didn't seem to have heard her. 'Well this is our time.' He thumped his chest again. 'Bandits time. And nobody better get in our way.' The chair legs scraped loudly on the lino floor as he stood. 'Be seein' ya, Nan.'

She heard him stomp down the front steps on his way out, his footsteps quickly fading. She sat and sipped her black tea. It was cool enough to drink now.

Bad things had come to her little town, she knew that. And worse was yet to come.

I t felt strange to Gemma, having other women taking over some of her normal duties. Sandy and Jenny had settled into running the house so quickly that she almost felt like a guest in her own home. Even her Dad was in on it, tending to the vegetable garden. She had to admit, though, that he did a good job – she had learned from him.

As soon as she had woken after her first night home she had been itching to get into the kitchen or the garden, to tidy up, to do something that felt normal. The better part of a week living rough, fighting their way home, had left her feeling disconnected from the home she had burned to get to.

Normal life was out the window. Mark and her Dad went everywhere armed, there were too many people in the house, and so many things had just got harder. Cooking, cleaning, washing up. It was like a camping nightmare. Looking out the bedroom window, she could see that the lawns needed mowing and the edges needed trimming. Archie was out there, collecting eggs with Jenny. He looked happy, but he should have been at school.

She sighed and ran her hands down the thighs of her black jeans. The jeans were clean, her long-sleeved green and black checked shirt was clean and smelled fresh. The white singlet beneath the shirt was soft on her skin. The wash she had had the night before – albeit it from a pot of hot water – had been the best wash she'd taken in a long time. She had washed her hair and scrubbed her skin and nails, shaved her legs and brushed her teeth for the first time since last leaving home for work. The lift it had given her had been incredible, and with a full stomach from a real meal, she had fallen into a deep sleep.

Standing in their bedroom now, she wondered how long this situation would last. How they would all come out of it. It wasn't like there was a nuclear war – the country had suffered major disasters before and got through. That was even the slogan for the Civil Defence campaigns they had – used to have – on TV; Get Thru. Fortunately, she and Mark had taken that a few steps further, and had been better prepared than most.

Nothing had prepared her for the life and death situations she had faced though. She'd told Mark and their parents about that last night, how she and Alex had been forced to defend themselves, the shootings and fights they had been in.

Her mother had cried and her Dad had even got emotional. Mark had held her and listened and Alex had chipped in to the story too. They had shared some of their own stories, but it had ended up very late and she knew there was more to come.

She looked over at the floor beside the dresser, to the holstered Glock she had been carrying. It had been on her or in her hand constantly the last few days, and it felt like she should be putting it on again. She looked out the window again and saw Archie and Jenny coming back from the chicken coop with eggs. The beefies had been moved and all the animals had been fed.

Gemma looked at the pistol again. Maybe not today. She headed to the kitchen.

Entering the sleepout, I leaned my Rossi lever action against the wall by the door and took a long drink of water from a bottle I had left inside. The manual labour of blocking off the road had been satisfying.

Alex came in behind me, leaning his rifle beside mine.

'So what's the plan here?' he asked, looking around.

The external walls of the sleepout had been reinforced with ply and stacked bricks, timber and bags of anything-we-could-find. The idea had been for us to have a safe room we could hunker down in if we were under attack – which we had been – with some protection from flying bullets. The original plan, before things turned to shit, had been for the sleepout to be fitted out properly as a bedroom with a small bathroom.

'We're getting pretty full inside,' I said, 'and we may still have more visitors.'

He gave me a surprised look. 'You think so?'

'Gemma's sister and her family may turn up. We contacted them but they reckoned they were going to stay put.' I shrugged. 'Apparently they thought I was over-reacting, but who knows, they could still turn up.'

'I don't think you were over-reacting.' Alex's face was serious. 'If you hadn't got hold of Gemma, we'd probably still be stuck back in the city. I don't know what I would have done if she hadn't been there.'

'You would've done what you needed to do,' I said. 'People under-estimate themselves.'

'I don't know...'

'You do now.'

'What?'

'You know now,' I said. 'You know what you can do.'

'It's Gemma that got me through it,' he said. 'I'd have been screwed without her. I'd be dead.'

'And she probably would be too, without you,' I told him. 'I know how much you looked after each other.' I stepped over to him and put out my hand. 'Thank you.'

We shook hands, and he looked away, quickly wiping his eyes. I pretended not to notice.

'Gemma tells me you were quite handy with that rifle,' I said, gesturing towards the Marlin leaning against the wall.

'Not really, I made it up as I went along,' he said. 'She showed me how to use it though.'

I smiled, feeling a swell of pride inside. Guns had never really been her thing, but she'd obviously listened when I'd taken her out shooting.

'Want me to show you a few things?' I said, and he nodded.

'That'd be good,' he said. 'If things continue the way they are, it'll probably be handy to know.'

I picked up the carbine and handed it to him. 'Unload it first.'

He dropped the magazine out then looking at me expectantly.

'Cool, so first off is the cardinal rule of safety; treat every gun as loaded. Is that gun loaded?'

'Um...' He looked at the Marlin as if it might tell him. 'I took the ammo thingie off...'

'The magazine.'

'Yeah, that. Um...yeah, I think so.'

'Okay,' I said. This was going to take some time.

Over the next hour, I taught Alex the safety rules, showed him the relevant parts of his weapon, and ran him through loading and unloading drills. By the end of the hour he was loading and unloading the weapon properly, had stopped waving the barrel around and was using the correct terminology. He was a fast learner, even though I could tell that guns weren't his thing. There was still plenty left to teach him, but we took a break and headed inside for morning tea, like we would on a normal day.

The others all wandered in too and we ended up scattered around the lounge, eating the last of the home baking and sharing a thermos of coffee. Gemma and Alex hadn't had hot drinks while they were on the hoof, and I shared mine with her after she had emptied her cup. She sat close to me on the two-seater couch, Archie on her lap with his legs across me. Rob and Jenny shared the three-seater with Alex, and the cat curled up on his lap, purring loudly as he stroked it. My mother took the armchair, commenting about her sore feet needing a rest.

'It's all this standing,' she said, 'I'm not used to doing so much housework when I'm not at home.'

I groaned inside and felt Gemma nudge me surreptitiously. We let that one slide, but I knew there was a line in the sand and my mother was approaching it at speed with no thoughts of braking.

'How's the diesel looking, Rob?' I asked, eager to change the subject.

'Fine,' he said. 'Still plenty there. When d'you want to run the genny again?'

'How about later this afternoon? I think doing it at night is too loud, the sound carries pretty far.'

'It wouldn't keep anyone awake, would it?' Sandy said.

'No, but if people hear it then they know we have a generator,' I said. 'I doubt that many people do.'

Alex gave me a questioning look. 'You think they'll try and steal it?'

I nodded. 'Either that or they'll want to use it, or just be annoyed that we have one and they don't.'

'That girl next door, Amy,' my mother said, 'she gave me a funny look when she saw me hanging out the washing. I don't know if she heard the machine or not, but it got her thinking.'

'We need to be mindful of how desperate people will get,' I said. 'We're lucky, in that we have enough food and water at the moment. We have a generator so we can use some power. We can defend ourselves.'

'Not everyone can,' Alex said. 'It's pretty bad out there. You're lucky it's so quiet here.'

I gave a short, bitter laugh. 'Hasn't been so quiet all the time,' I said.

'Some bad guys came,' Archie piped up, addressing Alex. 'They were robbers. Dad and Poppa had a fight with them and beat them. And some of them came back and Gran shot one of them.' His face was serious. 'They ran away.'

Gemma gave him a squeeze and Alex nodded sombrely.

'That's good that everyone's here to look after each other, eh?' he said. He turned his attention to me. 'I see you've got solar panels. Has anyone else got any round here?'

'Probably,' I said. 'None in our road, that I'm aware of. Why's that?'

'I was thinking it may be possible to hook more up and create a power bank. You'd need batteries of course, to store the electricity.'

'You know how to do that?' The idea appealed but I had no clue how to put it into practice.

He shrugged. 'I'm an IT guy. I'm sure we could figure it out somehow.'

I nodded, my mind starting to tick over. A knock at the door interrupted us and I swung Archie's legs off me to get up. He came with me to the door.

Rusty stood there, with a jar of honey in his hand. He handed it to me with a smile.

'Wow, thanks,' I said. 'What's this for?'

'From our own hivesh,' he said, his Dutch accent thick. 'I know you have housheful.' There was a strain to his smile when he ruffled Archie's hair. 'You might like it for your toasht, hey?'

Archie grinned and gave him a high five.

'Thanks very much Rusty,' I said. 'You want to come in?'

He shook his head and gave a strained smile again. 'No thanksh. Shophie ish at home, I jusht popped over.' He caught my eye. 'Have you had shomeone come round ashking for food?'

It was my turn to shake my head.

'I don't know who they are,' he said. 'They came just before, wanting to know if we any shpare food we could give them.'

'Did you give them any?' My alarm bells were ringing.

'I gave them a little, maybe one meal.' He shrugged. 'We're doing okay ourshelvesh, and she had a child with her.'

'A mum and a child, just them?'

'Yesh.'

'Who are they?'

'I don't know. She shaid her name wash Olive. I ashked where they live and she shaid around the corner.'

I frowned. It sounded dodgy to me. I wouldn't have given them any food, but I could understand why Rusty and Sophie had. Problem was, it made them a target for a return visit, and that concerned me.

'Did they go anywhere else?'

He shrugged. 'I don't know. I shaw them go back up towardsh the corner, sho maybe not.' He turned and took a step before looking back at me. 'I jusht thought you should know.'

I nodded and watched him go. For a man who was normally spritely, he was carrying a big load on his shoulders. I scanned the road in both directions but didn't see anyone, aside from Amy crossing the road to Bevan's place. I wondered what was going on there, but didn't really care. Nothing to do with me.

The others looked at me expectantly when I returned to the lounge. Archie had already showed them the jar of honey, and he had gone off to his room. I could hear him reading a Tintin book out loud to himself.

I filled them in on what Rusty had said.

'Interesting,' Rob said.

Gemma gave me one of her looks, the sort of look that said she knew what I was thinking and didn't approve. Problem was, I wasn't actually thinking much. True to form.

'And?' she said, arching an eyebrow. 'What're you planning to do now?'

'Well,' I said, reaching for my cup, 'I was going to finish this, then go and have a look at the sleepout again. Didn't really get started with that.'

She gave me her don't-jerk-my-chain look. I knew it well.

'You know what I mean,' she said, 'but I'll say it anyway. I don't want you going off and investigating these people. Just let it be.'

'I wasn't planning anything,' I protested.

'You don't need to,' she said firmly. 'You just do it without thinking – you can't help yourself.'

I shook my head and took a sip, but she was right and we both knew it.

8

The stolen Honda Fit was yellow and well-kept, and looked non-threatening.

The two fat girls in the front seats were dressed in their best tops and were excited to be part of the operation. Sindy, the driver, had a brother in Spring Hill, and was eager to see him again. Her cousin in the passenger seat, Lenore, was just happy to get out for the day.

They had been fully briefed by Little Dog and Pua, and were now advancing down the approach road towards the first check-point. Their job was to distract the soldiers there by talking, flashing some cleavage, and getting the soldiers' eyes off their surroundings. This would allow the boys to sneak in closer and attack the prison.

'We can do that,' Sindy had assured the gangsters with a laugh, 'we'll work our fuckin' asses off, yo. Can't turn this shit off.' She and Lenore had cracked up, and even Pua had managed to crack a smile.

Little Dog hadn't smiled. He had other things in mind for these girls.

Now, ten seconds out from the checkpoint, Sindy wasn't so confident. Even with the meth buzzing through her – that was some great shit these dudes had – the sight of several soldiers with machine guns unnerved her.

'Be cool,' she muttered to herself, 'be cool.'

'All goods, girl,' Lenore said, glancing at her. 'You need to, you gunna take some dick?'

Sindy felt her spirits lift. Lenore had a habit of keeping things simple.

'Maybe,' she said. 'But pro'ly only some head.'

'I'd take it all,' Lenore laughed.

'Shush now, we're here.'

The hatchback eased to a halt several metres out from the checkpoint, where a soldier was indicating them to stop. A second soldier was pointing a rifle at them from the other side of the road. Both looked alert.

Sindy buzzed her window down.

'Get your hands on the dashboard,' the soldier barked, and both girls jumped, doing as he said. 'State your business.'

Sindy couldn't take her eyes off the gun he was pointing at her. It was big and black and looked mean as shit. She managed to find her voice, but it came out as a squeak.

'I...we...fuck, bro...ah, we come...'

'Got a message,' Lenore said, jumping in to bail her out. 'Gotta talk to your boss, bro.'

'Two things,' the soldier growled. 'I'm not your bro, and you're talking to me. What's your business here?'

'I tol' you, we got a message,' Lenore insisted. 'It's important, and I don't mean to disrespect you mister, but we gotta give it to the boss. Your colonel or whatever.'

The soldier's eyes narrowed.

'Stop fucking about,' he said. 'What's this message? Tell me now, or we detain you right here.'

Lenore looked at Sindy. Her cousin seemed to have calmed a bit now. Sindy shrugged.

'May as well,' she said. She looked at the soldier. 'It's a message from the guys who come yesterday, the Bandits?'

The soldier made a scoffing sound. 'Oh yeah?' He'd seen their corporal, Shinks, run those fuckers off. Somehow he wasn't surprised they were trying again.

'Yeah. They said...'

At that moment, hidden three hundred metres away behind a hill, Dion flicked a switch on the remote control he held.

The explosives in the boot of the car exploded with a deafening boom, vaporising the occupants and the two soldiers standing near it. Shrapnel scattered far and wide and the high explosive pressure wave knocked the other soldiers flat behind their roadblock, scattering debris everywhere and shattering every window out of the Pinzgauer they had parked behind their post.

A massive cloud of smoke and dust roiled angrily before rising skyward.

9

The city below them was a smouldering wreck, some buildings still burning and some lying dead, smoking hulks of blackened, twisted framing.

Columns of smoke curled skywards, filling the air with the stench of burning – buildings, bodies and vehicles. The gas fires had burned out, thank Christ. Mickey pitied the poor bastards down there, the civilians and emergency responders, struggling to survive in the hell-hole the city had become.

Reports were coming in steadily of looting, rioting, raping and pillaging. Hospitals and liquor stores, gun shops and supermarkets were all being targeted. Emergency services personnel were under constant attack. The military were deployed on the streets under the provisions of martial law. They were supposed to restore order and keep a lid on the shit that was boiling away, but it was like waving a wet bus ticket at a charging bull.

They were hopelessly outnumbered and had their hands tied by the rules of engagement they were operating under. It reminded Mickey of the stories he'd heard of the Brits patrolling Northern Ireland way back when. *Do not fire until fired upon...there must be a clear and present threat.*

Screw that, he thought, as he looked down from the open side of the A109.

The chopper was buzzing back from the North Shore, passing over the Waitemata Harbour. Usually a picturesque flight, today he could see more than one oil slick on the surface where boats had gone down. The wreckage of one was still visible, and the Harbour Bridge was blocked with wrecked and abandoned cars.

He glanced back towards his colleague, seeing Glen snapping pictures on his long lens. The loadmaster was helping him identify points of interest. The intelligence was important, used for guiding the deployment of resources.

Mickey would have preferred to have been on the ground, confronting the problems head on. Or at least up high somewhere, sniping targets of opportunity. The big .50 calibre Barrett M107A1 was ideal for that – effective to a klick and a half, and he had hit targets at a full click with it in Afghanistan.

It was there purely for dealing with any material threats they came across, not for hunting; his OC had been clear on that when he'd paired Mickey up with Glen from Intelligence. He was there to protect the team, not put them at risk.

Mickey had kept his opinions to himself. Close to two decades in the Special Air Service and still a Corporal by choice, he knew his time was nearly up and not just due to length of service.

His opinions were often out of step with the way the military thought these days. Even the SAS, the crème de la crème of the Army, was going the same way. Too many young guys focussed on being tacticool, not tactical; too many fish heads kissing arse to get their next posting; too much political interference.

Mickey hefted the Barrett in his lap and peered out the door again. The pilot orbited off the bridge so Glen could get some live footage, then headed towards the city centre. They were almost done for the flight, and would be back at Papakura camp soon. Hopefully they would be out again soon enough, rather than twiddling their thumbs at base.

A radio comm came over the net, and Mickey adjusted his

headset to listen. He was almost deaf in his left ear and the wind was coming from the right, so he missed it and had to wait for the pilot to repeat it.

'They want us to do a visual of Spring Hill,' he said, his voice crackling in Mickey's good ear. 'Two sections down there, can't get them on the net.'

Mickey nodded, feeling a sudden shot of adrenaline. It wasn't the most exciting task, but something about it got his sixth sense tingling.

'Roger,' he replied, and glanced over to Glen.

He was sitting back now and the loadie was back in his seat too, good to go. The A109 picked up speed and Mickey watched the city go by beneath them. No drama with getting flight clearance from the airport these days.

They should be there within minutes, swing round and drop back to Papakura for a cuppa and re-tasking.

Maybe, Mickey thought. Maybe.

10

'Holy fuckin' shit,' Jake said, staring at Dion with wide eyes. 'What the fuck was in that?'

Dion shrugged. 'A few bits and pieces,' he said. 'I had some stuff lying around.'

Jake stared at him in amazement. He knew the guy had worked in the Aussie mines and did time over there for blowing safes, but this was something beyond his world. He was glad for the cover of the hill they were behind.

'Let's go,' Jake yelled, waving his arm forward like he was ordering the men out of the trenches.

He led the way on foot around the hill and across the open field towards the road. The Hampton Downs raceway was off to the side, and he could see the other boys already waiting at the top of the road in the vehicles.

Besides Dion he had six men with him, all armed and ready to go. When they got closer to the bomb site, he realised they would be going in easy.

What was left of the car was a few smouldering bits of metal in and around a deep crater. Sindy and Lenore were somewhere in the solar system. The soldiers had been blasted to pieces and all he could see, aside from one guy still intact, were pieces of meat and bloodied uniform dotted about.

An entire torso minus arms, legs, and head lay on the shoulder of the road, held together by body armour. Jake walked past it, almost laughing he felt so giddy from the blood rush.

He walked over to the only soldier he could see in one piece, the Steyr ready in his fists, but there was no need. The guy was bleeding from every orifice and his eyeballs were hanging out. Jake put a couple of rounds into him anyway, just for the hell of it.

He turned and waved the vehicles forward.

Little Dog buzzed down the window of the white Range Rover as it pulled up beside him, surveying the destruction.

'Motherfucker,' he breathed. 'That is some fucked up shit.'

Jake climbed in the back of the black Ranger truck that came alongside.

'Let's go,' he shouted.

The Ranger led the way and they rolled on down to the main car park. An Army ute was parked by the entrance gates and as soon as the column on trucks and hogs got closer, a single soldier stepped out with his hands in the air. With him was a uniformed prison officer. Neither of them was armed.

Jake covered them with the Steyr as he dismounted and approached.

'How many soldiers are here, bro?' he called out.

The soldier was a young Maori guy, barely out of his teens. The screw was older, a fat white guy with grey hair and a moustache. Jake thought he recognised him.

'Just us,' the soldier said. 'Me and the guys out front.'

'Better not fuckin' lie to me, bro,' Jake said, pointing the Steyr at his face. 'I'll fuckin' waste you right now.'

'He's not lying,' the screw piped up. 'Just him.'

'Fuck up.' Jake shifted his aim and blew the screw's head off with two shots. Blood spattered the young soldier and the body dropped.

'Fuck yeah!' someone cheered behind him. 'Bandits forever!'

Jake eyed the young soldier, who still had his hands in the air but was showing no sign of fear. He moved closer, ignoring the dead prison guard.

'You got everyone locked inside?' he said.

'Maybe half,' the soldier said. 'A bit more. Some escaped.'

'So what you doin' here?'

The soldier eyed him. 'Guarding it.'

Jake chuckled. 'Doin' a shit job so far.'

'Yeah?'

Gunfire erupted and a hail of bullets swept across the assembled Bandits and their vehicles, dropping three of them immediately and sending the others scrambling for cover. The young soldier snatched a pistol from the back of his waistband and fired as he backpedalled towards the gate.

Jake hit the deck and rolled, scrambling towards the Ranger. A bullet struck the Steyr and ripped it from his hand. More bullets punched into the Ranger above and around him.

He heard a Minimi open up, his guys shooting, like the whole world had erupted. He got in behind a wheel of the Ranger and tried to catch his breath. He couldn't hear himself think. A grenade exploded and someone screamed. More shots sounded.

He peeked around the wheel and saw the young soldier trying to open the gate to get back inside the compound. Bullets raked him from behind and he danced like a spastic before collapsing to the ground.

Jake felt himself grinning, and he looked around for the Steyr. It lay a few feet away, and he could see the receiver was damaged. He pulled out the Sig instead and poked it round the truck tyre, firing blindly towards the prison. The volume of fire was easing but the Minimi was still going hard, smashing the prison or whatever the gunner was looking at.

It took a few minutes before the boys stopped shooting, and Jake got to his feet. No bullets came his way but the air was thick with burnt cordite. He could see bodies around the vehicles and one of the hogs was on its side.

One of the boys was writhing on the ground, whimpering and

trying to hold his guts in. Before Jake could say anything, Dion stepped over and put a bullet in his head. The whimpering stopped.

Every wall of the prison in sight was peppered with bullet holes, the wire fence was holed in places, and a pair of soldiers lay dead on the grass just inside the fence.

Silence had fallen, broken only by the excited chatter of the boys, pumped as fuck on adrenaline and gun smoke.

'All good, boys?' Jake called out. 'Huks, Ricky, Black Jim – you fullas go have a look. You know what to do.'

He waited while the three nominated Bandits went through the gate into the prison grounds. He picked up the Steyr and checked it. A bullet had smashed into the receiver and twisted it, jamming the chamber. He tossed it aside, and took out a smoke instead.

Dion sidled over and bummed a smoke off him. Jake squinted through the smoke as he fired up Dion's ciggie with a disposable Bic.

'That's some pretty fuckin' mean shit,' he said.

Dion grinned and took a drag. 'Eh,' he said. 'Fucked it up alright, cuz.'

It took over half an hour to get all the remaining prisoners out, and they assembled in the car park. Jake stood on the back of the Ranger and had the boys cover them to make sure no one tried any funny shit. The odd shot had sounded from inside while the boys were getting them out, and Huks had explained that they'd come across a few screws and some members of opposing gangs, who'd had a go.

Once everyone was out and under guard, Little Dog and the rest of the boys came down.

Little Dog joined Jake on the back of the Ranger, all patched up and shades on and looking mean as fuck.

'Listen up,' he called out. 'You all got your ass rescued by the Bandits. You all know who we are.'

There were nods and murmurs.

'Any of our boys here?'

'Over here, boss,' Dion called out. He had pulled all the Bandit inmates to one side.

Little Dog jerked his thumb over his shoulder.

'Come over with the boys,' he said, and looked around at the rest of them. 'Any other clubs here?'

No one said a thing, and he grinned wolfishly. 'May as well say it now, coz if we find out you fuckin' lied, we'll fuck youse up.'

Jake noticed a small group of white boys gathered together at the side, standing out with their mullets and skinheads and swastika tats. He pointed towards them.

'Devil's Slaves,' he said. 'Boys?'

The boys were on them fast, dragging them out to the front, over-coming the pushing and pulling with kicks and punches. The five dudes looked around them, knowing they were fucked. Five white power dudes surrounded by a sea of brown faces.

'On your knees,' Little Dog said.

'Fuck you, nigger,' one of them snarled, and spat at him.

Dion and Pua opened fire at the same time, chopping all five of them down in a bloody heap. The other prisoners ducked and backed up as bullets ricocheted around the car park.

Little Dog looked them over.

'Last chance,' he said. 'If you wanna run with us, step up now. You wanna go on your own, we ain't stoppin' you.'

A voice sounded from somewhere in the throng.

'How we know you won't just shoot us, we leave?'

Jake spotted the guy, a skinny dude with dreads. Looked like fuckin' Snoop Dogg but with more meat on his bones, not so raggedy-assed.

'Give youse my word,' Little Dog replied. ''at's all.'

Snoop shook his head, not happy. He said something to the guy beside him.

'Come out here,' Little Dog said.

Snoop pushed his way forward until he was in the clear, facing the Ranger.

'You don't trust me?' Little Dog said.

'Ain't I don't trust you, man,' Snoop said. 'Course I trust you. But I got two years to go my time, man. I don't wanna part o' killin' screws an' shit, man, or 'scapin' prison, man. I got kids an' shit.'

Little Dog spread his hands, non-threatening.

'Up to you, my bro,' he said. 'Stay here if you want. Walk away if you want. I don't give a fuck.'

While that conversation was going on, Jake spotted a guy in the crowd who was deliberately keeping his head down, avoiding any eye contact. Only one reason a man did that. He pointed the guy out to a couple of the boys and they pushed into the crowd, going for him.

The guy tried to melt away into the sea of prison-issue grey sweats and green T-shirts, and a few dudes around him tried to shield him. No dice. The boys grabbed him and dragged him out. As soon as the dude looked up, Jake recognised him.

He grinned, but it wasn't a welcoming grin. The guy was named Jug, on account of his large ears, and he had been inside when Jake did his last lag. Jake had got busted with contraband in his cell – smokes, a little white, and a phone – and word was that Jug had narked him out. Jug got transferred the day after Jake was busted.

'On your knees,' he said.

Jug shook his head but the boys forced him down, holding him down by his shoulders.

Little Dog deferred to Jake, who looked over to where the Bandit inmates were.

'Eh, my bros. Come.'

They came forward, six of them, looking wary. Jake pointed at Jug, who was watching and waiting, his face telling the story – he knew he was fucked. Jake said one word.

'Nark.'

With that, the six Bandits were on him. The boys holding him stepped back and let them go for it. It was short and brutal.

Kicks, stomps, punches; all hell rained down on Jug and the best he could do was try to curl up and protect himself. It did no good. Freed from the confines of prison and the rules that went with it, and with a point to prove to their bros, the six men kicked Jug to death within two minutes.

Snoop Dogg melted back into the throng, deciding now was probably not the best time to make a stand on moral grounds.

When they were done, Jake got down and checked the man himself. No pulse and his head was swelled up like a misshapen balloon. Jake unzipped and pissed on his dead body, bringing a cheer from the boys watching.

Little Dog thrust his fists in the air and roared, 'Bandits forever.'

His boys were joined by some of the inmates, 'Forever Bandits.'

Jake zipped up, turned and grinned up at Little Dog. Even if they only got half these dudes, it was shaping up to be a good day.

With guns, cars and plenty of foot soldiers, they would be unstoppable.

11

W e were cleaning the dishes after lunch when I saw the people out on the road.

I put down my tea towel and looked closer, seeing a woman and a child come to the end of our driveway and stop.

'Have we got visitors?' my mother asked, putting the next clean plate in the dishrack.

'Looks like it.'

I picked up my rifle on the way to the door and called out to Alex, who was outside with Sandy.

'Watch my back, mate. I'll go see what they want.'

They slowed when they saw me coming and we met halfway. The woman was in her late twenties, with dirty blonde hair, a ring through one nostril and tats on her hands. She was dumpy and her T-shirt was loose enough to show a deep cleavage. The girl with her was close to ten, with long mousy hair and dirty clothes. Dumpy like her mother. I couldn't see anyone else around, no overwatch ready to drop me.

'Hey there,' the woman called out, giving a smile big enough to reveal a couple of rotten teeth. 'How ya doing?'

I stopped and waited.

'What are you after?'

She laughed like I'd cracked a good one.

'Gee, you're quite the character, aren't you?' She tried to mimic me. ' "What are you after?" Funny.'

The little girl laughed too, but I noticed her eyes never left me, sussing me out. I didn't laugh.

'Since we're neighbours, and I got the little one here,' the woman said, 'I just come round to say hi and see how you're all doin', and share a bit of love in the world, y'know?'

'Oh.' I gave her surprised. 'So you're not asking for food then?'

'Gee.' She nudged the girl. 'He's just straight to the point, isn't he?'

'Yeah.' The girl looked up at me with brown eyes that had no humour in them. They were eyes that had seen things a little girl shouldn't see, and there was an emptiness behind them. 'You're funny.'

Her gaze unsettled me. I'd dealt with kids like her before, and the pain they carried always came back to the parents. I didn't see a dad, and that was no surprise. I turned my attention back to the mother.

'So if it's not food you're after, how come you're out door-knocking?'

She tried to maintain the easy-going, we're-all-friends-here schtick, but I could tell she didn't like my manner.

'Things're getting tough out there, eh?' she said. 'We're just being neighbourly and checking on people, making sure everyone's okay. Anything wrong with that?'

'Not so much,' I said. I stared down at the daypack over her shoulder, where the zip hadn't closed properly. I could see a bag of apples inside. She shifted the bag further behind her. 'It's just funny that I know you were asking the people across the road for food. And now you're saying you're not...'

'You calling me a liar?' she snapped. 'Besides, everyone knows you got plenty in here – even got a generator.'

I must have looked surprised, because that made her smirk.

'Yeah, people hear it. They say you even got a washing machine goin'. So you're all high and mighty with me...'

'Stop,' I said coldly. 'Time for you to go.' She looked set to argue, and I stepped forward into her personal space. 'Now.'

We eyeballed each other for a long moment before she took the girl's arm and started to move.

'Come on Regan, I think we'll go. Leave this man to himself. Fuckin' fascist anyway.'

I was pretty sure she didn't really know what a fascist was, but I let it slide for now. I walked them down the drive to the road, the woman muttering all the way about me being a fascist prick and I better watch myself.

'Know what?' I said, when we got to the road. I could see Clyde walking towards us from his place. 'Just a heads-up.' The woman looked at me. 'The last people that tried to break in here got shot.'

'You fuckin' threatening me?' she said, acting up for the approaching audience. 'You're threatening to shoot my daughter? Oh my God, I can't believe you said you'll kill us.'

'What?' Clyde broke into a trot. 'What's going on here? Mark?'

'He said he was goin' to shoot us,' the woman told him, looking about ready to cry.

'Mark, come on,' Clyde chided me when he got to us. 'They're just people in need. I thought you were better than that, but you're getting out of hand.'

I raised my eyebrows but said nothing.

Clyde was getting into it now, and I could see the woman was enjoying it. She'd loaded the gun and he was firing it.

'You're not the sheriff round here,' he said.

'Finished?' I said.

Clyde put an arm around the woman's shoulders in case I was about to explode. I saw the little girl smirking at me, unseen by Clyde.

'I never threatened them,' I said, 'and I don't have to explain myself to you, Clyde. I'm not having beggars coming to my door, and that's that.'

'But Mark,' he pressed. 'These are *people*, your *neighbours*.'

'Funny,' I said, 'because I've never seen them before.' I jerked my thumb back towards our house. 'And I already have people to look after.'

Clyde shook his head sadly, and the woman actually managed a sob, even with dry eyes.

'I can't believe your attitude, Mark,' he said.

'Oh well, I'll live.' I turned to go home, then paused and looked back at the woman. 'Don't come back,' I said.

I left them standing on the road and walked up the driveway, seeing Alex standing ready with his carbine.

'What was that all about?' he said when I reached him.

'Trouble,' I said. I stopped and looked back to where they still stood, Clyde doing his social-worker-best. 'And I think they'll be back.'

12

The *whupp-whupp-whupp* of rotor blades carried on the wind and heads started to turn.

Jake scowled at the sky, shielding his eyes to try and spot the chopper. Whoever it was, they were using the sun at their backs to hide in.

'Is it cops?' Little Dog called out, craning to try and see.

'Na, it's the fuckin' Army,' Dion said.

'Air Force,' Pua said. 'Army don't fly helicopters.'

'Who gives a shit?' Dion retorted. 'Got guns an' shit, don't matter who they are.'

Jake finally got a decent angle and spotted it, a lone chopper standing off and watching them like a bug hanging in the sky.

'What the fuck do they want?' he muttered to himself.

Little Dog shot him a look. 'We just wasted some of their guys,' he said slowly. 'Maybe that's it, eh?'

Jake felt himself flush at being made to look stupid. 'I mean what're they gunna do? They comin' to have a go, or they just lookin'?'

The answer came when they saw a dude in the back move to the open side door. He raised a rifle towards them. Even at the distance and with the sun in their eyes, plenty of the gangsters and escaped prisoners saw it, and immediately began to stampede like a herd of startled cattle.

Guys were going down and being trampled over as they all scrambled for cover from what was sure to be a withering hail of lead.

Someone loosed off a burst of fire in the vague direction of the chopper and it brought more fire, wild shots ringing out. Jake ducked down behind the Ranger beside Little Dog, cursing the stupidity of the men that were shooting. He heard a Minimi opening up, and saw one of the boys over near the fence, firing it from the hip like he was goddamn Rambo.

Somebody even whooped and cheered him on. Jake shook his head and shouted, 'Knock that shit off! Stop firing!'

The next second the guy's chest took an impact and his back exploded open in a massive red spray. He fell back and stopped firing.

'Holy fuck,' Jake breathed. 'That was some shooting.'

'THAT WAS SOME SHOOTING,' the pilot said over the intercom. 'Holy shit.'

Mickey didn't react, concentrating on sweeping for more targets. If he'd had his way they'd have opened up and rinsed the lot of them down there. He could see the smouldering hulk of the Pinzy and the detonation site beside it.

He knew the boys down there were dead, wiped out by this bunch of shitbirds, and he wanted nothing more than to return the favour. He could easily pick them off either from the A109 or closer in if he could talk the air force boys into dropping them down. 450 metres out in a chopper was not ideal conditions, and he was quietly happy with his shot.

'Mickey.'

The marksman glanced to Glen, who was angling past him with his long-lens camera. Mickey leaned back, lowering the Barrett .50 to give him a better view. They were far enough away that it was highly unlikely any of the gangsters below would be capable of hitting them.

The guy with the Minimi had been a target of opportunity too good to pass up, even though he knew it would take some explaining later. Even in the Special Forces, bosses didn't like you drilling bad guys on home turf. This was supposed to just be a recce, not a direct action. The assault on the ground troops changed that, and Mickey knew what needed to happen.

'Good to go, fellas,' came the pilot's voice through their headphones.

'Rickety-tick,' Glen replied, sitting back.

Mickey scanned again through the scope, hoping for another suitable target. 'Hold up,' he said into his headset mic. 'We need to get some troops in here.'

'There's no one to rescue, mate,' the pilot said, his voice tinged with sympathy. 'They're gone.'

'We're not leaving,' Mickey insisted. 'We can get some troops here in thirty minutes. Hold off and maintain obs while I make a call.'

'We're running on fumes already,' the pilot came back. 'I've requested another crew to buzz down here, but we gotta put down soon, or we're going down.'

'Put me down first.'

'Sorry Mickey.' The chopper angled away as the pilot spoke. 'I know what you're saying, but we can't do anything for the boys. They're gone mate, and I don't want us to be as well.'

Mickey's gut knotted and his hand twitched towards the Glock strapped to his thigh. Shooting the pilot would do no good, but all his instincts were screaming at him not to walk away. He felt Glen's eyes on him, and he knew he couldn't count on him if he went rogue. Glen was a spook, unlikely ever to be tested under fire.

'Fuck it,' he muttered, twisting in his seat to get a last look at the gangsters that were disappearing into the distance now. 'It's not over, motherfuckers.'

AS THE CHOPPER dropped from view over the horizon, Jake got to his feet.

He looked around to see men slowly getting up, some freshly-bloodied from being knocked down. A handful were legging it south past the prison, as if they planned on running to Huntly. He disregarded them and looked back towards where the Minimi-shooter lay. He was in a large pool of blood, the machine gun across his legs.

'Grab that gun,' Jake said to the closest Bandit. 'Let's go.'

Little Dog joined him, wiping his sweaty face with both hands.

'LD, you gotta get gone,' Jake said, feeling calmer now. 'I'll get these dudes moving, but you gotta go 'fore they come back.'

Little Dog nodded his agreement and moved towards the white Range Rover with Dion and Pua.

'See youse back there,' he called out the window as the Rangey tore off with a pair of hogs as outriders.

Jake turned back to the rest of the boys, and climbed up into the back of the Ranger to get their attention.

'We goin' back to Meremere,' he announced. 'You get a ride if you can find room, else you walk it, unnerstand?'

No one voiced any disagreement.

'Get there and we'll get you fed and have a smoke, see what's up. Unnerstand?'

A few nods, and he jumped down.

'Mount up,' Jake shouted. 'Let's go.'

13

Bevan was raising a good sweat as he pounded the punch bag hanging in the woodshed, landing blow after blow.

Each hit ebbed away a fraction of the emotion that was swirling inside him, a combination of anger and self-loathing. Anger at that fuckin' faggot Alex for taking the piss out of him; self-loathing because he knew that Alex knew the truth. Truths that Bevan had hidden deep down for a long time.

Jab, jab, hook, hook. Jab, jab, hook, hook.

He knew he'd over-reacted towards the guy, but he couldn't help it. He was always bubbling close to the surface anyway. The humiliation he'd felt was damn near overwhelming, though. If Mark hadn't been there he'd have torn the prick apart.

Jab, jab, cross, elbow. Jab, jab, cross, elbow.

Bevan was far more self-aware than most people would have guessed. He knew they all saw him as the classic loner, the single man in his thirties, blue-collar job, liked guns, socially awkward. The stereotypical David Grey type, never destined to rise to great heights. He knew all this, and he knew they – the people in the community – were mostly right. People like Mark and Gemma had it together; they were good at life. Bevan had never been good at life, and he knew it. Goddamn, he knew it.

Jab, jab, cross, uppercut. Jab, jab, cross, uppercut.

He paused a minute, letting the bag swing as he caught his breath, the blood pounding in his head. His hands and wrists were humming and hot sweat was running freely down his bare chest. The bag creaked on its chain as it slowed to a gentle swing.

Bevan stripped off his gloves and began unwrapping his hands, walking outside as he did so. He heard approaching footsteps and glanced quickly to where the AR-15 rested against the shed wall. The dog hadn't barked, so either it was a friend or the dog was dead.

He saw Amy appear around the side of the house and he relaxed. He bundled the wraps together and waited as she approached.

'Been busy?' she said, running an eye over his taut, sweaty torso.

'Boxing,' he said, his breath still laboured. It had been a while since he'd hit the bag and he was feeling it.

'Are you good?'

Bevan frowned, unsure. 'At boxing?'

'Mmm.' She nodded. 'Are you good at fighting?'

Bevan considered the question for a moment before giving a short nod. 'I can hold my own.'

She blinked and nodded again. She looked at the ground for a second then back at him.

'I need help,' she said.

Bevan began folding the sweaty wraps in his hands. 'Yeah?'

'I need to go home,' Amy said.

Bevan felt a kick in his chest. He'd got used to having her and the kids around the last couple of days or so. They were good company; they talked to him. The kids even listened sometimes when he told them stuff about farms and country living; he got the feeling their own Dad didn't know much about that side of life, even though they lived rurally.

'Why?' he blurted. 'He won't be there.' He saw the enquiry in her eyes and he felt his cheeks go red. He shut his mouth abruptly.

'I know,' Amy said softly. 'But we need things. We didn't bring much with us. The kids need stuff, their own stuff.'

'So you mean go and get your things and bring them back here?' Bevan wiped a forearm across his face, clearing some of the sweat away. The day was that kind of cloudy that was deceivingly hot.

Amy gave a slight smile. 'Yes, exactly. But I don't want to take the kids. I need to leave them here so they're safe, and I need someone to come with me, to drive me.'

She folded her arms across her chest, and Bevan couldn't help but notice that it pushed her breasts up. Her cleavage was unmissable above the low neckline of her T-shirt. He felt his cheeks hotting up again. He'd noticed her cleavage a lot lately, and she didn't seem to mind. He felt a thrill run through him. There was nothing wrong with him – this chick was openly flirting with him. He was all good.

'You asking me to be your driver and shooter?' he said, injecting a cockiness into his voice.

Amy smiled again. 'Yes. Is that okay?'

He tried to be all nonchalant about it, act like he wasn't fussed. He wasn't sure he pulled it off.

'Yeah, no worries,' he said. 'I can help out.'

14

'How long do you think this can go on?'

We were walking down the road when Gemma asked the question. With a houseful, we'd needed some time together so had done a stint on guard at the roadblock. The Macklin farmhands had replaced us and we took our time wandering back home. Maybe this was the modern version of date night for married couples.

I sucked my bottom lip to help me think. 'No idea,' I said. 'Gotta be quite some time, given what's happening. I can't see it being all sorted before the end of the year, put it that way.'

It was April now, already into autumn. The end of the year seemed a long way off yet.

'Uh-huh.' Gemma pondered this for a bit as we walked. 'How long do you think we can go on?'

I glanced at her. She slipped her hand into mine.

'As long as it takes,' I told her, and squeezed her hand. 'We'll be fine. We'll stick together and look after each other, and we'll ride it out.' I gave her a smile. 'We'll be fine, we'll get through.'

Gemma nodded her agreement. 'Yep, just gotta stick together. I just hope Archie will be okay, and our parents.'

'Even Jenny?' I said with a grin, and Gemma chuckled.

'She hasn't been too bad,' she conceded. 'Funny how things change when the pressure comes on.'

I didn't spoil the moment. Sometimes you need to have your rose-tinted glasses on to make the view better.

'The wee man'll be good as gold,' I assured her. 'Our job is to protect him and nurture him, and he just loves being at home and having everyone around.'

'Poppa's little shadow,' she agreed.

We walked on a bit, nearly home now but both of us slowing down as if we were reluctant to actually get there. It was like the short break of a stint on guard duty was a break from reality, even though we were both armed.

Despite it being ugly and heavy compared to more modern weapons, Gemma had taken to the M3 "grease gun" and had it slung across her body. She hadn't fired it yet; that was something we needed to do. She needed to be confident if she was going to carry it, plus we needed to know it actually worked.

I made a mental note to do that as a priority. Seemed like everything was a priority right now.

'What about those beggars?' she asked. 'Do you think they'll be back?'

'No doubt,' I said.

'And if they do come back?'

I shrugged. 'Can't just shoot people for begging, or even really for stealing, if they pushed it.'

She gave me one of her looks.

'Really? Did you just say you can't shoot someone for stealing?'

I hiked my shoulders and said nothing.

'This is the man who wanted to set out road spikes when some idiot was racing up and down our road.'

'He was pissing me off. Besides, I didn't actually do it.'

'Didn't you shoot at a guy the other night for swearing at you?'

I frowned. 'He threatened us. Slight difference.'

'Hmmmph.'

We reached the driveway and crossed the cattle stop.

Gemma tugged my hand to stop me. 'We will be alright, won't we?'

Despite the ribbing she'd just given me, it was clear that she was actually concerned. I looked her in the eye.

'Yes we will,' I said.

'And if someone tries to harm our family?'

I paused. We both knew the answer to that, but she needed the confirmation.

'We kill them,' I said.

15

Papakura Military Camp was a hive of activity at the best of times, but the last week had gone nuts.

People buzzed about, choppers and vehicles were coming and going, and troops were deploying on small team jobs. As soon as the Agusta had landed, Mickey and Glen had made their way to the SAS HQ. Rennie Lines, known as "the compound", was a secure base within the camp itself.

Glen shot off to the Int cell, and Mickey went straight to the A Squadron hangar. The lads had all been staying on base the last few days and his troop had a corner set up for themselves with camp beds and tables set up. He heard his name called as he was dumping his kit by his bed.

The Squadron OC was striding across the hangar towards him, the Troop Commander in tow. Major Wood was a tall, imposing figure with the square jaw and chiselled looks of a Hollywood star. That had led to his nickname of Hollywood, which he publicly scoffed at but privately revelled in.

Captain Long, known as Shorty both for his surname and the fact he was short, was much quieter and was struggling to find his feet in his first posting within the unit. Mickey didn't have a lot of time for him, or for officers in general.

'Boss.' He ran a hand through his hair and grabbed a water bottle from beside his bed. He took a long draught and looked to the OC expectantly.

'Great int on Spring Hill,' Hollywood said brusquely, planting his hands on his hips and putting his shoulders back.

Mickey thought it would be a pretty good pose for GQ or M2. In the unit's hangar it made him look like a twat.

'There's a team there now,' the OC continued. 'Unfortunately all our boys are KIA, and the place is shot to shit. Looks like their Pinzy was blown up with a vehicle-borne IED of some sort. A few prisoners are dead, too. No great loss there though.'

Mickey nodded and wiped a dribble of water from his beard. He saw Shorty watching him, and the Troop Commander looked away quickly. Mickey disregarded him and glanced back to Hollywood.

'The lads have seen a lot of activity in and around Meremere,' Hollywood continued. 'They took some incoming when they had a recce so they've backed off and are dropping in a team for a CTR.'

Mickey nodded. A close target recce made sense, but would ideally be in darkness given the enemy – whoever they were – were armed and had numbers.

'You will deploy back there,' Hollywood told him, and Mickey's ears pricked up. 'No doubt you'll be keen to get amongst it.'

Mickey capped his bottle and tossed it onto his bed. Things were looking up.

'Shorty?' Hollywood turned to his subordinate.

Shorty stepped forward so he was beside the OC, licking his lips nervously before speaking.

'Yes, thanks sir...'

Mickey rolled his eyes. Nobody called the boss "sir". It was "boss" or nothing, at least to his face. Shorty caught the eye roll and licked his lips again.

'Yes, ahh, so you'll need to grab a team, another three guys,' he bumbled. 'Kit up, two days' initially, and head on down there by road.'

'Is there a free wagon?' Mickey interjected.

'Ahh, yes...yes there is...ahh, yes, so liaise with Sergeant Guptill,' Shorty continued. 'He's on the ground.'

'Got it.' Mickey gave a short nod, his usual indication to officers that he'd heard them and they could fuck off now to whatever it was they did.

Shorty took the hint and stepped back. Hollywood gave a broad grin.

'Top shot today, Mickey,' he said, flashing a brilliant set of pearly whites. Probably had them whitened. 'How far? Four hundred?'

'Bit more,' Mickey said.

'Bloody good,' Hollywood grinned. 'Love to hear a bit more later. Anyway, come on, Shorty. Things to do.' He threw Mickey a thumbs-up and turned away. 'Really top shot.'

Mickey started hunting out his gear.

'Top shot,' he muttered mockingly. 'Really top shot.' He grabbed his pack. 'Dickhead.'

Twenty minutes later he was out on the tarmac, slamming the tailgate on a bronze-coloured Nissan patrol. It was a brute of a wagon with chunky off-road tyres, bullbars, an assault platform on the roof and non-standard skirts for assaulters to stand on.

The back was packed with kit and the other three lads were loading up. Like him they were all in standard multi-terrain camouflage kit with body armour and their personalised webbing. Everyone carried a MARS-H 7.62mm long and a Glock 17 short, with a mix of grenades and other ordnance.

Turk was behind the wheel. Hump and Gazza got in the back. They were all good operators, Turk having been in the Middle East with Mickey, the other two being newer to the unit and not battle-tested. Given more time he probably would've taken other guys than Hump and Gazza, but they needed to roll.

Mickey climbed into the front passenger's seat and shut the door. He slid on his shades and turned to Turk.

'Let's cruise.'

Turk gave a nod and moved off, giving it some juice as he approached the gate.

Mickey felt a little kick of jazz. This was what it was all about – heading out with the boys to smash some shit up.

16

'Caleb and Mandy are coming to stay,' Archie shouted as he ran up the driveway. Jethro was bounding along beside him, his tongue lolling out in the wind.

I paused with my arms full of dry clothes from the washing line.

'Says who?'

'Rusty says,' he panted, reaching and leaning over with his hands on his knees. 'They're coming to stay with them, over there.' He pointed behind me in the rough direction of the Van Dijk's.

'That's okay then,' I said. 'Why?'

Archie straightened up, sucking down breaths. "cause their mum's going to get some stuff from their place, some toys and stuff.'

'Uh-huh.' I groaned inwardly. Going out there on her own was asking for trouble. Another problem I would have to sort out, no doubt – not that it was actually my problem.

He followed me into the garage.

'When're they doing that?' I asked

'I dunno. Today, I think.'

Gemma and Sandy were in the garage, appraising our food stores for maybe the millionth time. Food was a major consideration just now. Sandy took the washing from me and went inside, Archie trailing behind, no doubt planning to schmooze of one of his grand-parents into letting him have a snack.

'What're we going to do when this runs out?' Gemma said.

'We've got the beasts, and we've got fruit trees and a veggie garden,' I said. 'We'll be okay.'

'What about Rusty and Sophie?' she said.

'They're not doing too bad,' I said, although I knew they weren't as well stocked as us. They also only had the two of them to feed.

'Didn't you say something about a storage place in Mercer?'

I nodded. One of the benefits of my job was knowing strange things that were of no use to anyone until they really were.

'I think we should get whatever's there,' she said. 'At least we can share it with the Van Dijks, and whoever else.'

'Who's the whoever else?'

She shrugged then crossed her arms. 'I'm pretty sure not all the neighbours are doing as well as we are.'

I knew she was right, but my priority the last few days had been protecting my family. Everybody else came a distant second. I said nothing and she gave me a pointed look.

'I know what you're thinking,' she said, 'but if we're going to get through this we need to have support. And I know some of the neigh-bours have pissed you off – well, Clyde and Elette, anyway – but most of them are good people. The more people we have looking out for each other and pulling together, the better off we'll all be, won't we?'

I groaned inwardly again. Of course she was right; it was common sense, and had long been a standard approach in the prepper world. Mutual support and all that. Problem was, I didn't have a lot of patience with people. My circle of friends was very small, not much wider than my actual family.

'So you want me to go down to Mercer, risk my life to do a burglary, then come back and share the goods with people I don't really like?' I said.

Gemma reached out and patted my cheek, smiling.

'Exactly. Just stay safe while you're doing it.'

'Huh.' I pulled a face. 'Easy for you to say. I'll take Alex with me.'

BEVAN EASED the ute out onto the road and straightened up before getting out. He left the engine running and his AR-15 in the cab.

Sarge nudged against him, confused as to why he was being left at home. Bevan scratched his head and waited while Amy came down the road from the Van Dijks' place.

'All ready?' she called out cheerfully.

'Yep. I'll just go tell Mark then we're off.'

He turned to get into the ute again, but Amy stopped him.

'Why're you telling him? You don't need to check in with him, do you?'

Bevan paused, unsure.

'Na, but...you know.'

She shrugged as if she didn't care, and opened the passenger's door.

'Whatever,' she said. 'I just didn't realise he was the boss around here.'

Bevan climbed in behind the wheel.

'Yeah, I mean he's not, but...you know.'

Amy said nothing as he drove down to the Dobsons' place, passing her kids in the Van Dijks' front yard, talking with Sophie.

The old ute rattled over the cattle stop and trundled up the drive.

Mark and Gemma came out of the garage, watching them as they pulled up. Bevan wound his window down and Mark came over.

'I'm just running Amy back to her place,' he said. 'Gunna pick some of their stuff up.'

'So I heard.'

Mark looked past him to Amy, giving her a nod and a curiously appraising look. Bevan didn't like the look. Always the bloody cop.

'How long're you gone for?'

'Over and back today. Shouldn't be too long.' Bevan looked to Amy for confirmation but she said nothing. He turned back to Mark. 'Uhh...yeah. Not long.'

'Hang on a tick.'

Mark stepped back to talk to Gemma, who listened a moment then went inside. He came back to the window.

'We'll tag along to Mercer,' he said. 'I want to go do a recce there.' He gave a grin. 'Safer in numbers, eh?'

'Uh-huh.' Bevan watched as the other man moved off to the garage, feeling Amy's displeasure without even looking at her.

The other guy came out, Alex the gay one, with his rifle. He glanced over at Bevan then quickly looked away again. Bevan felt his anger rise just at the sight of him and he grit his teeth.

Alex went and got in Mark's truck and Bevan turned to Amy. The sour look on her face told him all he needed to know. He ground his teeth together and turned the ute around, ready to go.

17

M ercer was just a small settlement, most of the residents living in the wider catchment area. The service centre had always been busy but the workers there mostly travelled in from Te Kauwhata or Tuakau.

Coming down the road into town I could see that not much was going on – nobody was about and no vehicles on the road. It was quiet and still, just the birds chirping and the trees rustling in the wind.

Even the motorway, usually a constant hum of noise, was dead. We passed houses that were either empty or had people hunkering down inside. A mangy looking dog wandered across the street ahead of us, barely giving us a glance before disappearing into a yard. I kept my eyes everywhere behind my shades, wary of being ambushed for our weapons or food or just out of pure meanness. Alex took it easy but I could tell he was nervous.

Amy and Bevan were behind us in his truck.

'Stop short of the overbridge, mate,' I said.

The bridge and the highway were the high-risk areas for us, and with so few of us, discretion was our best defence. Alex pulled up short and I debussed, scanning around us until I was happy to go forward. I trotted down to the bridge, pausing to listen before checking over both sides at my end. Nobody seemed to be waiting for us, so I carried on across, waving the trucks forward once I'd cleared to the other side.

The chaos of vehicles on the highway below didn't look like it had changed since we'd last been there.

Bevan pulled up beside me and Amy got her window down.

'All good?' I said.

Amy looked apprehensive, but she nodded.

'Yes, and thanks,' she said. 'I hope the kids behave. We should be back by tonight.'

'Should be,' I agreed. I'd noticed her off-hand attitude earlier, but she seemed to have changed her tune now.

Beyond her, Bevan gave a nod.

'Come on,' he said, 'let's get moving. I don't like sitting around here in the open.'

I patted the windowsill. 'See ya later. Good luck.'

Amy gave me a nervous smile and the truck moved off, heading onto the bridge across the river that would take them towards her home. I wondered for a moment what they would find there. Hopefully it was good for her. Maybe her husband had made it home and was waiting for them, eager to be reunited.

Maybe.

I climbed in beside Alex again, and guided him to the right, towards the service centre. Before reaching the actual centre itself and the gas station beyond it, there was a tiny fire station, a Dutch cheese shop – world famous in these parts – and a couple of other small businesses. The fire station was empty and I presumed the crews had probably gone up to the city. The small businesses had all been ransacked, and I hoped that the place I wanted had escaped any attention.

Alex followed my instructions and pulled the truck over to the side of the road, facing back the way we'd come in case we needed to get out fast.

We debussed and scanned again, but nothing was moving.

'It's very quiet,' Alex commented, and I nodded.

'I hope it stays that way.'

I led the way on foot past the cheese shop, which was part of a small block of individual buildings butting up against each other. What most people didn't know was that there was another building between them. A narrow alleyway gave access between the buildings, the ground there littered with paper and trash that had blown in. I followed the alleyway to the other side, looking out towards the car park and the service centre.

Nothing caught my eye so I backtracked halfway and stopped by a wooden door set in a blank concrete wall. There was no external handle, just a simple tumble lock, and the door appeared to be undamaged.

'This is it,' I said. 'Cover the other end and give a shout if anyone comes.'

Alex did as he was told and I unshouldered my day pack. I selected a pry bar from the tools inside and set to jemmying the door open. For once I was pleased that a client hadn't followed my security advice. After they'd been burgled here, I'd recommended a steel grill door, heavy duty locks and cameras. None of it had been implemented, but it made my job easier now.

The jemmy made short work of the lock, splintering the frame as the door popped open.

I lit up the interior with my torch and felt my heart lift. My guess had been right – the storeroom was untouched. It wasn't a massive store, but it was well-stocked. There were boxes stacked on boxes, all clearly labelled and appearing undamaged. Tinned foods, boxed dry goods, bottles of sauces. Bottled water and soft drinks, packets of condiments. Confectionery and potato chips and baby food. Even toilet paper and tissues.

I backed out and went to Alex, tucked in at the mouth of the alleyway to keep watch.

'We're all good,' I said. 'Back the truck up to here and I'll load it up.'

I covered him while he did so, then left him on guard while I lugged boxes from the storeroom and stacked them in the back of the Navara. It was hot work and before long I was sweating freely. After about ten minutes the truck bed was nearly covered, and I swapped with Alex. I rehydrated while I stood watch, and he puffed and strained with the load. He wasn't the most physical guy around, but he stuck at it and we swapped again.

By the time we'd finished, the truck was fully loaded up and we were both sweating and ready for a break. Fortunately I'd taken the canopy off at home, making it easier to load.

'Can you secure it?' Alex said, watching me close the door.

'I can only close it. If someone else finds it they can help themselves, I guess.' I left the door closed as best I could and wedged it shut. I was heading back towards him when shots rang out.

We both ducked instinctively, but I could tell the crack of the bullets was some distance away. I joined Alex beside the truck, scanning for threats, and it wasn't until another volley of shots sounded that I saw them.

A police patrol car had come north up the highway and was stuck behind a pile-up of wrecked vehicles. I could see two blue uniforms behind it, facing back south, both firing rifles at a target I couldn't see. They were taking a lot of incoming fire, what sounded like fully automatic rifles firing in bursts. I could see the patrol car taking hits, and the volume of fire they were taking told me they were about to get their arses kicked.

'Come on,' I told Alex, 'we need to help them.'

18

The drive from Mercer to Pukekawa was only a few klicks and they had made it uninterrupted.

It was nice countryside and looked undisturbed from recent events – sheep and cattle still grazed in paddocks, birds still soared and swooped, the wind still rustled the trees. If it wasn't for the fact he was armed and constantly looking for threats, Bevan would have thought things were back to normal.

'Next left,' Amy said from the passenger seat.

He nodded and slowed. It was all rural roads here, no suburban build-up. Urban spread was years away from Pukekawa. He took the next left and cruised until Amy indicated a driveway on the right. He took it and pulled up outside a stylish two-storey grey house.

'This it?'

He put the truck in Park but left the engine running.

'Home,' Amy said softly.

She got out and hurried to the front door, fumbling with her keys and dropping them twice before she managed to open it. Bevan followed behind, casting an eye about, one hand on his AR-15. His senses were tingling but he wasn't sure why. He couldn't see anyone. Maybe it was just nerves.

He followed Amy into a house that felt cold and empty. The furnishings all screamed family home to him, the complete opposite of his own spartan, bachelor existence. Kids pictures and school notices on the fridge and the noticeboard. Toys in the lounge. Photos everywhere. Some of them were just the kids, some the family together.

The wedding photo in the hallway showed a younger Amy and a soft-looking man with thinning hair grinning at the camera, all loved-up. A more recent family photo showed that the man had chubbed out in the intervening years and had lost more hair, and Amy had also stacked on several extra kilos.

Bevan grunted to himself. The guy looked like a dweeb. No wonder he hadn't fuckin' made it. He realised he couldn't hear Amy anymore and he turned to look. She was standing just behind him, silently watching him. Bevan took a step back in surprise, wondering how she'd got up so close.

'Ahh...I was just...'

Amy waited silently, her dark eyes on his. For some reason his heart was pounding and he couldn't get his words out.

'I just...' He jerked a thumb at the photos. 'What's he do?'

'My husband?'

He swallowed and nodded.

'Alistair's in IT.' The dark eyes never wavered and she didn't smile. 'He's a brilliant man.'

Bevan nodded. His mouth was dry.

'I need to get some things,' Amy said. 'Wait here.'

Bevan nodded again, getting himself together. She moved to the stairs before turning and looking back at him.

'Don't go poking around,' she said.

Bevan gave her a thumbs-up and watched her disappear upstairs. He had no interest in poking around at all. In fact, all he wanted to do was get the fuck out of there.

19

R
ob had moved the cattle and partitioned off part of the paddock to keep them in. It used to be an electrified wire but hopefully the beasts didn't realise the power was off.

He had then fed the pig, who had come to the fence for a pat, snorting and blinking at him. He wondered if they would end up having to kill it for food, and how that would go down with little Archie.

The boy was inside playing Lego with his grandma – she was a difficult woman, but he had to admit, she was good with him. Sandy and Gemma were doing washing and whatever else needed doing inside.

Rob turned away from the sty and looked across the fields. Everything was quiet and still, like it always was in the country. It was a peaceful place and he had always enjoyed visiting here. It took him back to his childhood, a far simpler time. He wondered what kind of world Archie would grow up in. The violence of the last few days had been unbelievable. He had to think for a moment of how many people he had shot. Mark had well eclipsed that – the man had nine lives, thankfully. Rob couldn't remember the faces of the people they had killed, but they were there, following him around. He had no issue, at least in principle, with what he had done. But it didn't lift the black shadow that weighed on him.

Rob crossed to the shed, put the feed bucket back, and headed back towards the house. He was thirsty and hungry and tired. He hadn't been sleeping well and his mind was constantly working. If this was retirement then it could go to hell.

Hopefully the girls had some coffee on.

He paused for a second, the lightness in his head giving him the wobbles for a moment. He took a deep breath and unslung the old Lee Enfield, using it as a crutch while he got himself together. He took down another deep breath, trying to get his heart rate under control, but if anything the damn thing was getting faster. He felt a cold sweat break out on his face and he leaned harder on the rifle, his breath coming in short gasps. His chest felt tight and his legs went wobbly again.

The fence he was staring at started to shift and he took a step, tripped on the rifle and the ground rushed up to meet him.

20

Leaving the truck where it was, I ran across the car park and up the road towards the overbridge. The firing continued from the cops' position and also further down the highway, but it wasn't too far away. It sounded like at least three weapons, and they were going for it. I could also hear vehicles, the throb of big engines.

Reaching the overbridge, I dropped low and got to the steel safety barrier, giving myself a good view down the highway. Alex dropped in beside me, panting. About fifty metres away was a Ford Raptor truck with the doors open, facing towards us. A guy was shooting from behind each door and another two were up in the tray, firing over the roof of the truck. Another fifty or so back were two hogs with leathered-up bikies, revving their engines and cheering. Further on from them was another truck, maybe a Ranger, with more heads in it.

I had no idea what had happened, but I did know these pricks would overrun the cops with ease unless we helped them out.

'Stay here and when I start firing, put rounds down at the shooters,' I told Alex. 'Try and hit them, but at least stop them from shooting back if you can. I'll do the same. If things turn to shit we bug back to the truck and get the hell outta here, okay?'

'Got it.' He readied his Marlin, and I ran doubled over up onto the bridge, getting several metres between us.

I took a breath, got the Rossi butt into my shoulder, and raised up over the concrete barrier wall. The firing continued below us and nobody seemed to notice me. I took aim at the guys down at the Raptor, concentrating on the two in the truck bed first – they had the better angle with their height, so were the bigger threat to the cops. As I zeroed in, everything around me shut down and I came into a little bubble of my own.

I took a bead through the scope on the shooter to my left, who had what looked like a Steyr in his hands and was putting down rounds. I squeezed the trigger, the Rossi thumped and nudged back into my shoulder, and the guy jerked backwards, arms flying in the air as he fell on his back in the tray of the big truck.

I worked the lever and heard a series of pops from my right as Alex opened fire. Somebody shouted but I couldn't make out what they said. I shifted my aim to the second shooter in the back of the truck, who had stopped shooting and was staring at his fallen mate, seemingly confused.

He turned as I fired, and instead of blowing a hole in his shoulder blade, the .357 Magnum bullet ripped across his upper arm. I heard him scream as he staggered back, dropping his weapon and clutching at his wound. While I was still working the lever, someone else nailed him with a couple more shots and he fell on his arse in the truck bed.

Bullets started slamming into the concrete barrier wall in front of me, and I ducked down. I crabbed along to my left, listening to the sounds of the battle and trying to figure out who was doing what. I could hear the thump of rounds going down but it was all so close that I couldn't tell who was doing what.

I raised up again with the Rossi ready, seeing the driver of the Raptor had moved back behind the truck and was firing towards the cops below me. He was going for it with bursts and I zeroed in on him. I could see part of his shoulder and head as he leaned around the tailgate, and my first shot missed.

He didn't seem to realise and stayed where he was, which made the second shot easier. It hit his hand or weapon and knocked the Steyr to the ground. He ducked back out of sight and I turned to the guy on the other side of the truck.

He was out of sight but I could see his muzzle flash and puffs of smoke as he fired. Looking across the overbridge, I saw Alex changing magazines. He was lying down now, which was a sensible move, and had moved across to his right. For an IT geek, he was showing some good tactical sense.

He came back into the aim and started firing again, the pop of the Marlin's 9mm rounds a welcome addition to the thumping of the 5.56mm rounds from the cops and the bad guys below us.

I moved back towards him and pushed up once more, seeing the driver of the Raptor climbing back in behind the wheel. I punched a round through his door but he kept going, revving the engine as he got it in gear. The other passenger leaped in the back tray and the truck roared backwards. I sent my last two rounds towards the cab as a parting gift, then ducked back as more rounds thudded into the concrete wall and whizzed overhead.

Doubled over, I ran along to my left, paused to reload the Rossi, then sneaked a peek over the top. The guys back down the road had stopped giving covering fire and were heading south, the Raptor bringing up the rear.

Silence fell but my ears were ringing like crazy. The adrenaline and thrill of battle were urging me to give chase to them, but the little voice in the back of my head told me it would be suicide. Best to bug out now while we could. I trotted back to Alex, who was staring down the highway after the bad guys. We grinned at each other and threw a high five.

'Unbelievable,' he shouted, as deaf as I was. 'There must've been twenty or even more of them. I can't believe we won.'

'Better check on those cops.'

We made our way down to the car park, and could see the patrol car still on the highway. One cop was leaning against it, holding his arm and looking down. He saw us and struggled to grab the M4 on the bonnet of the car.

'We're the good guys,' I yelled, raising my free hand in the air. 'You guys okay?'

He waited for us and we climbed the barrier to join him. Brass bullet casings littered the ground around the car, both .223 and 9mm, and I could see he was bleeding from his left shoulder. His colleague was slumped on the asphalt, unmoving, blood soaking his uniform trousers.

The wounded cop looked at me with a mix of distrust and hope.

'Thanks,' he said. 'He's dead. The bastards shot him.'

'I'm sorry mate.' I knelt and checked the guy's carotid pulse. Nothing. I straightened up. 'We need to get moving before those guys come back. Are you wounded?'

'I think so.'

He showed us his shoulder, which was bleeding freely and had turned his sleeve and arm red. He had a decent open gash across the bicep.

I popped the boot of the patrol car and got out the red trauma kit. It only took a minute to wash the wound out with saline then patch it and strap it. Alex kept an eye out all the while, getting jittery as the adrenaline eased off.

'Come on,' he urged. 'We need to get a move on.'

'We're good,' I said. I was still amped and knew I would be for some time yet.

'Thanks for your help,' the cop said. 'Good luck.'

I did a double-take. 'We can't leave you here.' I indicated all the spent shells and his wounded arm. 'You're not in much shape to defend yourself, are you?'

He shrugged his shoulders and looked down at his dead colleague.

'I need to bury him,' he said, his voice thick with emotion.

'We'll bring him with us,' I said. 'Grab your gear.'

He nodded and looked relieved.

'Okay,' he said. He put out his hand. 'John Blake.'

We made quick introductions then Alex shouldered the trauma kit and I handed him the M4 dropped by the dead cop. Blake grabbed his own bag from the patrol car and I manoeuvred the dead guy onto my shoulder in a fireman's lift.

'Anything sensitive left here?' I asked, and Blake shook his head. 'Let's go.'

We made it back to the truck unmolested and I placed the body carefully in the back, rearranging the supplies to make room. We secured it all down with a cargo net and Blake gave me a look.

'Where'd you get all this?' he said, unable to hide his suspicion.

'Kind of a burglary,' I said with a grin, 'but it's okay, I know who it belongs to.'

'And?'

'Sort of a client.' I could see he was having second thoughts. 'Long story. I'm an ex-cop. Don't worry, we're not actual burglars.'

We got going, and left Mercer behind us. The houses we drove past were still closed up but I saw a curtain twitch in one and an old man stared at us from his front porch as we went past.

I kept an eye on the mirrors but nobody followed us.

21

'Here he is,' a soothing voice said.

It was somewhere in the distance. Light was pressing on his eyelids and he stirred. Rob gingerly licked his lips and cracked open his eyes. Sandy was watching him with concern, seated beside him on the bed. He could see her eyes were puffy and red.

Over her shoulder was Gemma, more composed. He lifted his hand and Sandy took it in hers, clasping it to her.

'You gave us a fright, Bobby,' she said, smiling tearfully. 'You silly fool.'

Rob managed to smile. She rarely called him Bobby, and she was the only one who did.

'It's alright, my girl,' he rasped. 'Drink?'

Gemma leaned over with a cup of water and a straw. Sandy held his head up so he could drink. He took a mouthful and leaned back on the pillows. The room wasn't familiar, and he definitely wasn't in the bus. He felt weak and closed his eyes again.

Sandy let Gemma take her father's hand so she could check his pulse.

'Looks okay,' Gemma said. 'He probably just needs to rest.'

'Is Poppa going to be okay?'

Archie had come into the room behind them, Jenny in tow.

'He needs to sleep,' Gemma said. She pulled her son in for a hug, rubbing his back. 'He's just a bit worn out and isn't feeling well.'

'Can I stay with him?' Archie looked up at her with big eyes, worry written all over his face. 'I'll be really quiet. I could bring him a teddy, that would make him feel better.'

Gemma smiled, her eyes prickling. 'Let's leave Nana with him,' she said. 'But you can bring him a teddy, I think he'd like that.'

Archie fetched one of his soft toys, a rabbit with long, droopy ears and tucked it in beside his Poppa. Then he gave the old man a soft kiss on the forehead and followed Gemma and Jenny from the room.

Sandy looked down at her husband, holding his hand and stroking it with her thumb. He looked old and tired on the bed, but he seemed to be breathing fine. He was a tough old rooster, so there was every chance he would come right from whatever it was that had dropped him. She didn't know what she would do if he didn't.

She closed her eyes and prayed to a God she hadn't prayed to in years.

22

'We're stationed at Thames,' Blake was saying. 'When this all kicked off we all got sent out on patrol, even me and Luke. I'm a community cop and he's in Youth Aid. We got sent over to Ngatea to help out there, there was only guy stationed there, but we lost radio comms and things turned to shit pretty quick when the power went out.'

'Same everywhere,' I said. He was sitting in the middle of the back seat so we could talk.

'Jobs kept coming in, people would turn up and tell us about being burgled or whatever, and we ended up running round like blue-arsed flies trying to keep a lid on things.' He shook his head. 'Wasn't working very well.'

'Did you get back to Thames?' Alex asked.

'Nope. We ended up in Paeroa, trying to help out there, but that place just went downhill real quick. Looting and shit everywhere, it was pretty bad.' He paused to look around the backseat. 'You guys got any food or water? I haven't eaten since yesterday.'

Alex passed him a water bottle and rummaged in my bag for a snack, coming up with a muesli bar and crackers. Blake took them gratefully and got stuck in, continuing to talk as he ate.

'For the last two days we've just been zipping around, helping where we could. People are getting pretty desperate but there are some good people around. We haven't been home since it started, haven't seen any other cops for two days.'

I glanced at him in the rear view mirror.

'Where've you been staying then?'

'Slept in the car last night,' he said. 'A barn the night before. The car the night before that. Haven't had much sleep though.'

I nodded.

'Where's home?'

'Thames, both of us.'

'Well, we'll get back to our place and get you sorted out. Bury your mate and get you fed and rested, how does that sound?'

'Sounds great.' He leaned back in the seat and I could see the strain in his body. His face was pale and drawn. He sighed. 'Sounds great.'

23

When Rob woke, Sandy was still sitting beside him, holding his right hand.

A stuffed rabbit was tucked in beside him and he realised he was in Gemma and Mark's room. A crocheted blanket was over him and he felt a presence to his left.

Sandy touched his face tenderly, stroking his cheek as he floated back to consciousness.

'Welcome back,' she said softly. 'How're you feeling?'

Rob turned his head towards her and ran a mental check of his body. He was lethargic and his head hurt.

'Not bad,' he said. 'What happened? I remember falling over.'

'I think you fainted, had a little turn.'

He nodded and licked his lips. Sandy helped him take a long drink from a straw then he laid his head back on the pillow. Sandy gestured towards his left with a smile, and he looked over. Archie was curled up beside him with the cat, watching him.

'Poppa?'

Rob lifted his arm and the little boy snuggled into him. The cat opened an eye lazily and purred.

'How long...?'

'About an hour or so.' Sandy squeezed his hand. 'You donged your head but it's nothing major. Gemma patched it up.'

He touched his forehead, finding a dressing taped there. His head hurt. As if reading his mind, Sandy popped a couple of Panadol from a packet and held the cup while he washed them down.

'Thanks.' Rob gazed at his wife, trying to keep his eyes open. Sleep was pulling him back down. 'I've had better days.'

'You might have a concussion,' Sandy was saying, but she sounded far away. Rob tried to speak but it was too hard. He held onto his grandson and his wife's hand and slid back down into the darkness.

WITH NONE of us being medically trained, patching up Blake's wound became a joint effort.

He sat in a folding chair on the deck while Gemma and I worked on him. The wound was washed and cleaned with antiseptic strong enough to make Blake wince, despite the hefty shot of whiskey he had downed. The bullet had split the skin and left a reasonable gouge, but we were able to close it up with butterfly strips then secure a breathable gauze pad over it.

Infection was the main concern now, but unfortunately we couldn't just pop into the A&E clinic. We'd have to make do with what we had.

Blake was pale and tired by the time we'd finished, and it was clear that the last few days had taken a toll on him. He happily accepted a bowl of hot soup from Jenny, awkwardly spooning it with his left hand. My mother sat with him while he ate and Gemma and I went back inside, where Sandy still sat with her husband.

Rob was drowsy but had some colour in his cheeks, which was a good sign. Sandy looked stressed and didn't protest when Gemma gave her another bowl of soup.

'It's only a packet,' Gemma said, 'not like your own, Mum.'

Her mother managed a smile and tried it. She put the spoon back in the bowl and looked at us with wet eyes.

'What am I going to do?' she said quietly. 'I don't want him to die.'

'He's not gunna die, Mum.' Gemma leaned down and hugged her. Sandy held on and cried. I rescued the soup before it dressed the carpet.

'Forty years,' Sandy sniffed. 'I can't lose him now.'

'You're not going to lose him, Sandy.' I put the bowl aside and crouched before her. 'He's a strong guy. Look at him.'

She did so, and she welled up again. I took her hands in mine.

'He'll get through this,' I told her firmly. 'He's just had a bit of a turn, and I'm not surprised. It's been stressful for all of us. This is not something any of us were prepared for, but we're getting through it. We'll have our blips along the way, and this is one of them.' I squeezed her hands and gave her what I hoped was a reassuring smile. 'He will be okay if we look after him, and we will.'

Sandy nodded through her tears and Gemma passed her the soup bowl again.

'Eat,' she said. 'You'll be no good to us if you fall over too.'

We sat with her while she slowly ate, and after a while Rob stirred. He opened his eyes and looked first at us then at Sandy. He smiled weakly when he saw his wife.

'My girl,' he said softly. He reached for her hand and she held it as they gazed at each other.

Sandy gently touched his face and spoke softly to him, helping him take a drink of water. Gemma and I slipped out to give them some privacy, and went to the kitchen to get lunch ready for the rest of us. Archie followed us inside and went back to playing with his Lego.

'Dad looks a bit better,' Gemma said.

She took bread from the pantry and a knife from the drawer. I put the bread board on the bench.

'I think he just needs rest,' I said.

I didn't say it, but I was hoping that was all it was. As usual, Gemma seemed to read my mind.

'We can't have him being crook,' she said. 'What the hell would we do with him then?'

'Get him to the Army,' I said. 'I'm guessing the hospitals are either closed or swamped.'

She nodded, and gestured towards the deck where Blake and Jenny were talking.

'What about him?' she said.

I shrugged.

'We can't just leave him out there,' I said. 'If he wants to go home or wherever, and I presume he will, then fine. No drama.'

'What if he wants to stay?'

She was serious and I understood why. I considered my answer, but really, there wasn't much to consider.

'While he's injured, I think we're kind of obliged to help him out. At least we know he's capable.'

Gemma gave a nod.

'I knew you'd say that,' she said. 'He's also another mouth to feed.' She sighed. 'It's only midday and already I've almost lost both you and Dad.'

She welled up and came for a hug. I held her close and kissed her head.

'It's okay,' I said. 'Your dad's going to be okay, and I'm still here, still kicking.'

'It's Archie,' she said. 'I'm worried about him.'

We pulled apart and she looked up at me.

'We can't leave him orphaned or without one of us. We need to be more careful.'

I agreed but didn't think I'd been careless. It probably wasn't the best time to be pedantic though, so I kept my mouth shut.

'We need to make a pact,' Gemma said. 'That we will always put Archie first and make sure he isn't left...you know.'

She didn't need to say "orphaned"; I got it. I nodded and tried another hopefully-reassuring smile. It wasn't my forte.

'Okay,' I said. 'I'll be more careful and we will always put Archie first.'

'Same.'

'We'll get through this,' I said. 'As a family – all of us. Whatever this is, we'll get through.'

Gemma leaned up and kissed me lightly on the lips.

'It's a deal,' she said.

24

The longer that Bevan spent in Amy's house, the more he realised he didn't know her.

They'd spent some time together in the last day or two, sharing personal details and talking, but the more he thought about it, the clearer it was that she hadn't really shared much at all.

While she packed bags upstairs in the bedrooms, he had checked out the ground floor living areas. Photos and knick-knacks always told a story, and Bevan had been around the block enough times to be able to read people.

He had two ex-partners and a daughter he never saw – wasn't *allowed* to see, thanks to her bitch of a mother – and had spent the last few years pretty much cutting himself off from people.

As far as he was concerned, he was just a normal guy who wanted to be left alone to do his own thing.

Amy on the other hand...her house gave him the creeps. She was a good-looking woman, smart, obviously had some money. She had said she was a teacher, and he saw evidence of that around the house – a framed degree on the wall alongside her husband's one, correspondence on the local school's letterhead.

Studying at the photos, he could see the forced smile she wore in every snap. The only photo he saw where she was actually loose with a full-on happy grin was one with the kids, taken on a beach somewhere. The three of them were walking hand in hand in a line, laughing together. It looked to be a couple of years ago and was taken in the late afternoon when the shadows were getting longer.

He put the photo frame back on the shelf and looked at the one beside it. Amy and her husband, Alistair, huddled together at some kind of formal event, maybe a wedding or a corporate dinner. He had his arm around her and was pulling her close. While Alistair hammed it up for the camera with a big cheesy grin, Amy was all stiff shoulders and a rictus smile.

That was a theme through every photo he saw of them together, and it made him wonder.

'What d'you see?'

The voice behind him made Bevan jump, and he turned. Amy was right there again, watching him. Her expression was almost blank, just the tiniest hint of amusement there. He hadn't heard her coming, and it unnerved him.

'Nothing, nothing,' he mumbled, trying to get his heart back under control. 'Nice house.'

'Mmm-hmm.' Her dark eyes gave nothing away.

'Did...have you...y'know?' Bevan licked his lips and swallowed. 'Have you got your stuff?'

'Mostly.'

Amy held his gaze for a long moment before abruptly heading towards the kitchen. Bevan heard a cupboard door open and containers being moved. He took down a deep breath and got his shit together. The AR-15 weighed heavy over his shoulder, a familiar, comforting weight. He listened to the kitchen drawers rattling.

Something about this woman was making him jittery, and he couldn't quite put his finger on it.

It took him a few seconds to click, but the silence spoke. The rattling of drawers and cupboards in the kitchen had stopped. The house was silent aside from his own ragged breathing. Bevan dropped a hand to the grip of the AR-15.

'Amy?'

Nothing. The kitchen was around a dividing wall from the living room. He couldn't see in without moving.

'You alright in there?'

Nothing. He moved as quietly as he could, his feet soft on the carpet but his gear creaking as he edged towards the kitchen doorway. He froze when he heard the rustle of clothing.

'Amy?' He put an edge in his tone now. His nerves were jumping like frogs on hot tin and he was afraid his voice would crack. For a moment, he considered making a run for it, getting in the truck and getting the fuck outta there.

'Bevan.'

'Yeah?' He was straining his ears to listen, but couldn't hear anything.

'Come here.'

She wasn't asking, but she didn't sound aggressive either. If anything, her tone was light, almost cheerful.

'What're you doing?' He swallowed and gripped the rifle tighter. His thumb rested on the safety catch, ready to flick it off at a moment's notice.

'Just come see.'

Fuck it. Bevan sucked in a breath and edged around the doorframe, staying well back just in case. He could see most of the kitchen, and it was clear. He edged round further, bringing the barrel up to cover.

Crossing the doorway, he saw her. Sitting on the benchtop to his left, her legs dangling free. She had a cheeky look on her face, her hair hanging loose, her legs bare.

Her top and jeans were on the floor, and she wore just plain white cotton knickers and a matching singlet.

'Come here,' she said, crooking a finger at him.

Bevan hesitated, not knowing what to say or do. The AR-15 felt superfluous in his grip now.

'I need some company,' Amy said softly, opening her knees. 'Come here.'

25

With Rob awake and now resting, and Blake asleep in the campervan, it was a good time to take stock of things.

I was still buzzing from the gunfight, and I needed some time to get my breath back from it. It seemed strange, having gone from a fairly peaceful life to having more gunfights in the last few days than I could immediately recall.

Alex was inside having a cup of tea and talking to Jenny, and I guessed he was decompressing in his own way. It was always good to debrief a critical incident, and I wasn't surprised when Gemma came out to join me. I put down the box of soft drinks I was carrying and she came in for a hug.

'This is insane,' she whispered into my neck, holding on tight. 'I'm glad you're okay – again.'

She pulled back and looked at me.

'I'm constantly worrying,' she said. 'Every time I wake up, every time I look out the window...every time any of us goes anywhere, even across the road.'

I listened. I knew what she meant, but I also knew it was different for her. It had always been like that; I went to work and did what I did, sometimes coming home battered and bruised. She fixed me up and I went back the next day, playing whatever cards I was dealt, leaving her at home to worry and hope for the best.

'Alex did well,' I said, 'he's got more balls than you'd think for an IT guy.'

'Changing the subject to distract me?' she asked pointedly, and I gave a half-shrug.

'Maybe a little,' I said. I pulled her to me again and held her close. 'It's going to be okay.'

'I hope so,' she said sincerely. 'Now stop flirting and get on with unpacking.'

Gemma and I unpacked the extra supplies from the truck into the garage, where we already had some of our supplies on the shelves.

Even though we both knew it was morally the right thing to do, having an extra mouth to feed would put more strain on our resources. We already had Alex, plus our parents. The initial run I'd done to the supermarket, back on the day that the national emergency had been declared, had given us plenty of supplies for our small family.

The longevity of those supplies diminished with every extra person that arrived.

The extras that Alex and I had just got bought us more time, probably another two or three weeks or so, but we both knew it wouldn't last forever.

'Who knows how long it'll be until things are back to normal though,' Gemma said.

She sounded optimistic, but we both knew there could be no certainty either way. With a Government who preferred setting up working groups and think-tanks than actually making decisions, it could be a long time. If we even had a functioning Government any more at all. We also didn't know how much damage had been caused further down country by the earthquakes, which was what had caused the national state of emergency in the first place.

'I'm not holding my breath,' I said. 'The more self-sufficient we are, the better. Our biggest risks right now are probably food spoilage and scavengers.'

'We should be okay with food not spoiling,' she said. 'The freezer's still okay with the generator, and we're managing our food so we're not wasting anything.'

'All credit to the ladies in the kitchen,' I grinned, using an old rugby cliché.

Gemma raised her eyebrows. She still wasn't comfortable with her kitchen being invaded by our mothers.

'Hmm,' she said.

'I guess Alex is staying us for the longer term?' I said, and she nodded.

'He doesn't really have anywhere else to go,' she said. 'Plus, I kind of feel I owe him a bit.'

Their time on the road together, battling to get home and stay alive in the process, had created a bond for them that would be hard to break. I got it, and I had no issue with him staying with us. I felt a debt of gratitude towards him too. Plus, with the way things were at the moment, it was handy to have another shooter around.

'I don't know about Blake yet,' I said. 'He may want to go home, but it's a matter of getting there safely. He shouldn't be going too far just yet, at least not until he can look after himself properly.'

'Fair enough,' Gemma said. 'D'you want a hand to bury the other guy?'

I shook my head.

'Just keep Archie distracted,' I said. 'He doesn't need to see that.'

Gemma went back inside and I headed over to Bevan's place, with Jethro in tow. He bounded along, sniffing and exploring places he'd sniffed and explored a thousand times before, and I carried the M4 front-slung. I threw a wave to Rusty across the road as I walked past and saw Amy's kids in the backyard there with Sophie.

I wondered how Bevan and Amy were getting on with their trip back to her place. Hopefully they would find her husband there, safe and well, and the family could return home. Hopefully, but unlikely. Probably they'd end up coming back empty handed and be back to square one. At least Bevan would be happy about that – he seemed to have taken a bit of a shine to Amy.

I got a strange vibe off her and Gemma hadn't warmed to her either.

Bevan's place was locked up and quiet, and I got to work. I'd dropped the body off there earlier, in order to keep it away from our place, and it was short work to load it up on the digger we'd borrowed from the Macklin place across the road from Bevan's.

The digger bumped and juddered across to the far corner of Bevan's paddock. We'd buried a couple of bad guys there before, and now I dug another grave. I took more care with this one, getting it deep enough that scavengers wouldn't burrow down.

That done, I lugged the body in its blue tarpaulin and slid it into the grave. I used the digger to fill it in, then patted the dirt down with a shovel and smoothed it over. Lastly, I hammered a steel waratah into the ground and, using baling twine, I lashed a cross-piece of scrap wood to it to fashion a cross.

I put the tools aside and stepped back. I didn't admire my handi-work, or say anything profound.

I thought of the cops I had known who'd passed on, of the cops I hadn't known who'd died in the line of duty, and of the cops I'd worked with who'd put their necks on the line to protect others. I said a quiet prayer for Luke, willing his soul to rest peacefully, knowing he'd gone down fighting to protect his community.

I'd been to Police funerals before, and had never enjoyed them. It was right to honour the fallen and to acknowledge their sacrifice and service, but it only brought home to me how vulnerable we were out there. I didn't want my family to be seeing me off like that – I wanted to die an old man, when my service was acknowledged as a part of my life, but nothing more.

So wrapped up in my thoughts was I, that I didn't hear Gemma approaching until she was beside me. She slipped her hand into mine and stood with me. The wind had picked up and brought with it the hint of rain coming. The temperature had dropped and the trees rustled and shifted.

We stood silently and bid goodbye to a man we had never known.

26

The house was silent as Bevan and Amy recovered their clothes and got dressed.

He couldn't quite believe what had just happened. Women didn't throw themselves at him, never had. And for it to happen in circumstances like this?

Mind-blowing. One for the ages.

Bevan shook his head again as he zipped up his pants. He sneaked a quick look at Amy as she pulled her jeans up her thighs. She wasn't wasting any time; job done, move on. She wasn't ugly and hell, who was he to complain? He knew he was no oil painting himself.

Besides, any sex was good sex, right?

He laced up his boots and stood straight, tucking himself in. He watched Amy adjust her top and run her fingers through her hair. She caught him watching and her cheeks coloured as she looked away quickly.

'What?' Bevan grinned. 'Don't be embarrassed, nothin' to be ashamed of. We're two consenting adults, right? Not hurting anyone.'

Amy straightened herself up and looked at him.

'I shouldn't have done that,' she said. 'I'm not like that.'

He shrugged and grinned again. 'Can't say it happens to me every day either darlin', but when it does, I don't say no.'

Truth was, he couldn't think of a time it *had* happened to him. Relationships had never worked great for Bevan, even casual ones.

He finished sorting himself out and reached for his rifle.

'Don't worry,' he said casually, all Mr Chill now he'd had his way. 'I won't tell anyone.'

'You better not.'

Bevan felt a jolt through his gut and his heart kicked up a notch.

Gone was the playfulness from her voice, the friendliness, even the tinge of uncomfortable awkwardness she'd just shown. All gone, replaced by a steely determination.

He paused with his hand half-way to his AR-15, glancing over his shoulder at her.

Amy was stood behind him, right up close. Closer than he'd thought she was. He could almost see the cogs turning in her head as she stared at him.

Her eyes were fixed and cold, and there was no emotion in her voice when she spoke. It was more than enough to make Bevan drop any thoughts of a repeat performance.

'You hear me?' she said. 'You better not.'

27

The coals in the barbecue were white and grey and the mutton chops and pork sausages were almost done.

Aroha stepped back again, a pair of tongs in her hand. She turned to the rickety outdoor table and picked up her beer. It was warm and flat but she drank anyway. Sometimes a warm, flat beer was better than no beer at all. She took a long draught and let it slide down easy. She was just calculating how many days she could make the barbecued meat last when Jake appeared around the side of her house.

'Hey, Nan,' he called out. 'Thought I smelled your cooking.'

'Come here, boy,' Aroha smiled, waving him over with her tongs. 'You wanna stay for some dinner?'

He grinned and stopped to kiss her on the cheek. He was different away from his gangster buddies, she noticed. This was the old Jake she knew and loved. Meal calculations went out the window and she sent him inside to get another plate.

They sat at the outside table on old chairs Aroha had scrounged when the school had a revamp.

'This from your garden, Nan?' Jake shovelled a fork load of watercress salad into his mouth and ate hungrily.

'Of course, Jake.' Aroha sliced off a piece of sausage. She would only have one tonight – two more were on Jake's plate, alongside a mutton shoulder chop. She planned to save the other chop for tomorrow. 'You know me and my garden. Nothing tastes as good as something from your own garden.'

Jake grunted his satisfaction and shoved down half a sausage.

'How're things, boy?' Aroha chewed on her mouthful and watched him as he ate. It was like he hadn't eaten for days. 'Everything okay?'

Jake nodded, pausing to wipe his mouth on his forearm. 'Yeah, all good Nan.' He gave her a half grin. 'Those boys not annoying you any more, eh?'

Aroha frowned. 'I don't like those boys being around so much, Jake,' she said carefully. 'Them and their loud motorbikes and guns, and their cursing and that P stuff. It's not good.'

Jake grunted and swallowed his mouthful. 'They're alright, Nan. Boys will be boys, eh?'

Aroha frowned again. 'I don't like it,' she said. 'Why d'you have to hang around with them, Jake?'

He ripped a chunk of meat off the chop and started to chew. 'Bandits forever, Nan. How it is.'

Aroha tut-tutted. 'That's not how you were raised, boy.'

He shrugged and swallowed. 'They're family, Nan. It ain't open for discussion.'

Aroha focussed on her food and said nothing for a few minutes. She knew when it was time to ease back with Jake.

'Jake,' she said finally. 'I need to know one thing.'

He stopped eating and looked at her, suspicion in his eyes. 'What?'

'How long will they be here for?'

Jake shrugged. 'Dunno. Long's Little Dog says so, I guess.'

Aroha nodded, knowing there was no point in pushing it any further. She crossed her knife and fork and pushed her empty plate away.

Jake grinned and patted her hand. 'We're gonna get some more food and shit, Nan. I'll make sure I bring you some, eh?'

Aroha nodded and smiled and put her other hand on top of his, giving it a squeeze.

'I wouldn't say no, Jake. Long as it's honest food.'

He frowned. 'Honest food? Food's food, ain't it?'

Aroha chose her words carefully. 'Where you getting it from?'

He grinned without humour. 'That guy that shot up the boys? Killed Henry?'

Aroha felt her heart go cold.

'We know where he stays. We're gonna go take his shit, get some revenge for what he done to us.' Jake frowned harder, seeing she didn't approve. 'Revenge is a bitch, Nan. Nothin' he don't deserve.'

Aroha sighed. No point arguing with him, no matter how wrong she thought he was. Wasn't just Jake anyway – that Little Dog and his hoodlums were behind him too. Bad news, the lot of them.

'And when're you doing this?' she said.

'Maybe tomorrow,' Jake said. 'Just gotta get a few of the boys sorted.' He wiped his mouth on his arm. 'Some of the boys ran into some trouble today, got shot up by some pigs. Ambushed 'em up at Mercer, shot the boys in the back when they wasn't even doin' anything.' He leaned to the side and spat angrily onto the grass. 'Fuckin' pig shits all the same.'

Aroha nodded again and left the subject alone. She was well aware of Jake's attitude towards authority; it was the reason he was what he was. She'd had her own scrapes with the law a long time ago, but that was ancient history now. No point raging through life. Besides, the Bandits getting shot up for doing nothing? Seriously?

Aroha kept her thoughts to herself. The germ of an idea was forming in her head and there was no way she could let Jake know it. He'd kill her if he knew. Or maybe not him, but one of them would. Of that she had no doubt.

The man who had come to the village, all fired up and ready to spill blood, had seemed like a decent man. An angry man, but decent anyway. She could understand his anger. She had heard that little punk Cyrus talking about what had happened at the man's house, when Donald – another little punk she didn't like – had got shot.

Putting that together with snippets she had heard from Henry and the others, she had a rough idea of where the man lived.

As soon as Jake took his leave and headed back to see his Bandits mates, Aroha started putting her plan together. It was helluva dangerous, but she didn't see any other option. She knew what the Bandits would do, and she wouldn't have blood on her hands.

She was too long in the tooth for that shit.

28

Heading out of Pukekawa gave Bevan a sense of relief.

He hadn't realised how unsettled he had felt at Amy's house. He couldn't put his finger on it; it just didn't feel right. It was like her mood had changed there, but he didn't know why. There was no reason for it to. They were just two adults going to pick up some belongings, two consenting adults who maybe got a bit carried away with each other.

He was still all buzzy about the sex, no doubt about that. It had been a long time. Amy didn't seem quite so jazzed about it, but he didn't push it with her. She'd gone all weird about it afterwards with telling him to keep his mouth shut, but whatever. She was married, after all. Probably just embarrassed.

But, wheeling along the empty country highway, Bevan knew it was more than that. Couldn't pin it down, but it was there. Sneaking a sideways glance at her, she was staring straight ahead. Expressionless. She felt his eyes on her and turned her head.

'What?'

'Nothing.' He tried a sly grin. 'Just looking.'

Amy didn't return the grin, just remained stony-faced. 'Keep your eyes on the road.'

Bevan turned away, his grin disappearing. The sun was warm on his face but he knew that wasn't why his cheeks were hot.

He felt a hand on his thigh but kept his eyes straight ahead.

'Hey.' She squeezed his thigh.

She was smiling when he looked over.

'Sorry for being grumpy,' she said, keeping her hand on his thigh. 'I didn't mean to be. Just stressed, I guess.'

Bevan licked his lips and said nothing.

'What we did back there was nice,' Amy continued. 'But it needs to be our secret, alright?'

He nodded, liking the feel of her hand on his thigh.

'I mean, I don't know what's going to happen,' she said. 'After all this is over, I mean. I've got the kids to look after, you know? I can't just be throwing myself at every man that comes along.'

Bevan tried the sly smile again, with what he hoped was a dash of boyish charm.

'I'm not just any man that comes along,' he said. 'I'm here to protect you.'

He cut his eyes over to her for a second, and looked into two dark pools. Bottomless pools that gave nothing away. He switched back to the road, his mouth dry again.

'Sure,' Amy said, the touch of enthusiasm sounding forced. 'I'd like that.'

Bevan concentrated on the road ahead. He was keen to get home.

29

The contents of the freezer should have lasted only a couple of days or so with the power out, but we had managed to prolong that by regularly using the generator. Now nearly a week into the emergency and we were still looking good, a hell of a lot better than most.

Still, it wouldn't last forever and food needed to be eaten. With that in mind, we had been carefully managing our meals and ensuring that we ate whatever was starting to defrost first. It led to some pretty patchwork meals, but everyone was getting fed, so there were no complaints.

Gemma had decided to do something special that night, and had got the old charcoal kettle BBQ out. We didn't use it often, preferring the speed of gas, but it was always memorable when we did.

A pork roast and a whole chicken had been defrosted and cut into pieces. The pork had been marinated in a tangy plum sauce, the chicken glazed with sweet chili. The pieces were placed in the kettle barbecue and left to cook for the afternoon. Every time I went near it, the smell had got my mouth watering.

She had resisted the help of our mothers, preferring to do it all herself. I suspected it was her way of stamping her mark, of reclaiming her kitchen. I don't think the two older women minded a break – cooking for all eight of us was no mean feat – and I could see that Gemma was happy being busy.

Come dinner time everybody was washed up and ready to go. Rusty and Sophie had come over to join us, seeming happy to get out and do something sociable. I hadn't seen Bevan or Amy since they'd got back earlier, and the kids were gone from the Van Dijks'.

I helped Gemma to serve at the outside table, and it was a spread to be admired. Aside from the pork and chicken, she had fresh potatoes, beans and peas from our garden, corn on the cob, and a loaf of her own sour dough bread.

It was a simple meal but, in our world, simple was usually best. Plates were piled high and there were murmurs around the table as everybody tucked in. I sat beside my wife and nudged her with my elbow. She looked at me and I gave her a wink and a smile.

'You did good,' I said and she smiled.

'You have sauce on your nose.'

I left it where it was. 'It's how we do it in Belgium. It's called a Belgian dip, *ja*.'

She chuckled at my Austin Powers movie reference and Archie laughed too, although he had no idea what we were meaning. He was too young for the Austin Powers movies just yet.

'This is fantastic, Gemma,' Alex said, grinning from the other end of the table. He had cleared half his plate already. 'Thanks so much.'

'More than welcome,' she said.

'In fact,' Alex said, raising his water glass, 'thanks to all of you. You've made me so welcome, and I can't thank you enough. Cheers.'

We raised a toast and clinked glasses.

'And good neighboursh, too,' Rusty added with a smile. 'We are very lucky to have such good neighboursh and friendsh.'

I noticed Blake was quiet, his arm wound making it more difficult for him to eat. I didn't know him yet, but it was obvious that he was feeling some serious pressure. I made a mental note to get alongside and spend some time with him, but it would have to wait.

Right now, I had some good eating to do.

30

G rowing up in the small towns and farms of North Waikato, Aroha had always walked to school or ridden a horse. In a poor family, riding a horse meant bareback, and that's how she travelled that night.

Waiting until it was near dark, she left her house by the back door and went over the low wire fence to the meadow beyond. There was enough light to make her way to the farm without having to rely on the torch she had brought. The evening was cool and she pulled her well-worn polar fleece jacket around her thin shoulders. The farm was run by the Maunsell family, distant relatives in the way that everyone around these parts were somehow related.

Aroha had used their horses many times, and usually it was an opportunity for a cup of tea and catch up when she wanted to borrow one. Tonight was different though. She didn't want to risk anyone tipping off Jake or his mates that she had come and borrowed a horse for a night ride. Such a move would bring questions she didn't want to answer, from people she didn't want to have to lie to. Such a move, she knew without a doubt, could be fatal.

So there would be no asking and no catching up. Aroha followed her internal GPS to the right paddock, knowing where the horses were kept. It was almost dark now, but her eyes had adjusted enough to recognise each of them by their shape and movements.

She was oblivious to the eyes watching her every move from a concealed hide a hundred metres or so away.

The animals heard and saw her coming and they stirred, curious as to the nocturnal visitor. Aroha clicked her tongue and came up to the fence, cooing to them to keep them calm and quiet. She didn't want any of the Maunsell family coming from the house, only a hundred yards or so away.

'Nellie girl,' Aroha cooed, holding out her hand. 'Come come, girl. Come come.'

The older grey mare wandered over and sniffed then nuzzled her hand and took the sugar cube from her palm. Aroha stroked the horse's neck and whispered soothingly to her. Nellie was the oldest of the Maunsell's horses, and was the one that Aroha rode most often.

Even though it had been a while since she'd ridden her, she knew Nellie was sure on her feet and not skittery like some of the younger ones. They would take good care of each other.

Two minutes later Nellie was out of the paddock and the gate was re-latched. Aroha smoothly hooked up the bit and reins she had brought with her, then climbed carefully up the fence railing until she was high enough. Nellie knew what to do, coming alongside and waiting patiently while the old woman climbed onto her back.

Aroha smiled to herself as she settled into place and gave Nellie a gentle nudge in the side with her heel.

Riding like this always reminded her of her childhood, the little girl who had explored the countryside on horseback, having more adventures than any of the boys she had grown up with. It was those adventures that led her to know the land like the back of her hand, every track and gully and ridgeline.

She gave Nellie a loving stroke down her broad neck and set off.

IT WAS deep in the witching hour when I was woken by the crunch of feet on the gravel driveway.

I stirred on the couch, cracking one eye open as I listened. Not just one person, but something different, maybe an animal. Who the hell would be riding a horse up our driveway at this hour?

I flicked my blanket away and rolled off the couch fully clothed, snatching up the M4 and moving bent over to the window. In the moonlight I could see a horse being led up the drive, almost at the house now, by Sean and one of Darren' boys. I knew they had been on guard duty down at the roadblock, so whoever it was on the horse must have come visiting.

I made my way outside and met them at the top of the driveway, as Darren's son was helping the rider down. Sean came over and spoke to me in low tones.

'She's come from Meremere,' he said. 'Says the gang there are going to come and attack us, probably today or tomorrow. She wants to talk to you.' He shrugged in the darkness. 'Well, I guess it's you. She asked for the boss guy that came down to Meremere and told them he'd kill them if they came back here.'

'Yeah,' I said, 'that'd be me.'

The old woman came over and extended her hand.

'*Kia ora*,' she said, clasping my hand. 'I'm sorry for disturbing you at this time, but I have some information you need to know. I can't let it happen, not in my heart. I wouldn't be a good person if I did that.'

I wasn't convinced yet that she wasn't a distraction or a spy, either gathering information or coming to keep us occupied while the gang snuck up and attacked. But something about her struck me as sincere.

I let go of her hand and looked closer at her. She was shivering and seemed frail.

'How long have you been out tonight?' I said.

She gave a half-shrug.

'Since just about dark,' she said. She may have seemed frail but her voice was strong. 'I been riding a while, eh.'

'Come in,' I said. 'Come and tell me what you need to tell me, and I'll make you a cup of tea. How's that sound?'

She nodded and I caught a glimpse of white as she smiled.

'Sounds good to me, mister.'

The Coleman camping lantern was strong enough to light up the lounge, and we sat close so we could keep our voices down.

The old lady gratefully accepted a hot cup of sweet tea, wrapping her bony hands around it and inhaling the steam it gave off. She didn't have much meat on her beans and looked about frozen, despite the fleece she wore.

She took a sip and savoured it, fixing me with her rheumy brown eyes.

'Those boys are mighty angry with you,' she said. 'Say they're gonna come and kill you and take what you got.'

She glanced around the lounge then back to me.

'Looks to me like you're better off than most folks,' she added.

I felt my hackles rise, as if she was taking a jab.

'Everything we've got we've worked hard for,' I said. 'Unlike those shitkickers.'

She gave a small nod. 'I was just stating a fact, mister,' she said softly. 'You are better off than most, and they know it.'

I felt my jaw set and forced myself to take a breath. She wouldn't have ridden all this way on a damn horse just to have a dig.

'When're they coming?'

'Soon,' she said. She took another sip of tea. 'Next couple days, I'd say. They gettin' more guns and things, I think.'

I frowned. 'More guns? Where from? What kinda guns?'

'One of them, the man in charge, he got a connection somewhere. They got all machine guns and things, real Army stuff I guess you'd say.'

I glanced at Gemma, seeing the concern in her face. This was not good news. There was no way our little enclave would survive an onslaught by a gang with military weapons. At best there were a handful of us who could use a weapon properly, and we had limited tactical capability.

'How're they planning to do it?'

Aroha shook her head. 'I don't know the details, mister.'

'Mark,' I said.

'Mark,' she nodded. 'I don't the details, but I thought you should know. I don't want no blood on my hands.'

'We appreciate you telling us,' I said sincerely. 'I know you're putting yourself at risk by doing this.'

She took a long drink of tea, sighed and looked at the floor.

'I'm just a old lady,' she said. 'I'm nothing to them, not even to Jake anymore. I used to pick that boy up when he fell, give him a bed when all the crap at home got too much.' She shook her head sadly. 'Now I'm nothing to him. Just a stupid old lady, worth nothin' to him no more.'

Gemma reached over and squeezed her hand. 'I don't know this Jake,' she said. 'But he's losing it by not appreciating you. You're a good person.'

Aroha gave a nod of thanks and patted her hand.

'I done some bad things in my life,' she said. 'But I never hurt an innocent family, and I ain't gonna start now. Just 'cause the world's all gone to hell, don't mean we have to go backwards, does it? We got to treat people with kindness.'

She looked at me again.

'That's why I tried to warn you the other day,' she said. 'I tol' you not to come back here, to my town.'

'Too late though, wasn't it?' I said. 'I'd already humiliated that guy – is that your boy, Jake?'

'That's him.'

Gemma raised her eyebrows at me. 'Humiliated him? Was that a good move, given the current situation?'

'I only humiliated him by staunching him out,' I said. 'I took a gun off him. It's not like I pulled his pants down and laughed at him.'

She gave me her *don't-be-a-smart-arse* look, a look I knew well. There would be plenty of time – hopefully – for reprimanding me later, but right now we had a goldmine of information at hand. I turned my attention back to Aroha.

'Tell me about these guys,' I said. 'Everything you can remember.'

By the time we ran out of questions, Aroha had finished a second cup of tea and had a peanut butter sandwich. She ate with the careful restraint of her generation, but it was obvious she was hungry. I wondered exactly how bad things were for her, and determined that if we could help her in some way, we would. First, we had to deal with the Bandits.

We helped Aroha onto her horse and walked her down to the road. Gemma bid her farewell then and I walked her to the road-block, the horse's hooves clip-clopping loudly in the darkness.

'Travel safe,' I said, 'and thank you.'

'Look after yourselves,' she said. 'God speed and *kia kaha* (stand strong).'

I patted the horse's flank and she set off.

'All good, Mark?' It was Sean, standing off to the side, watching and listening.

I blew out my cheeks. 'Hopefully,' I said. 'Got some planning to do though.'

GEMMA WAS WAITING for me when I got back inside. Sitting on the couch with her hands clasped together, she looked up at me, her face pale and pinched.

'What the hell are we going to do, Mark?'

The same thought had been racing through my head on the walk home. I perched on the edge of the sofa beside her.

There was only one option, but I didn't like it.

'I don't have any reason to trust her or not trust her,' I said. 'My gut tells me she's being straight up.'

'And?'

I considered my words carefully, not wanting to blow her anxiety through the roof.

'I need to go and have a look,' I said. 'And we need to be prepared to fight.'

If it was possible, Gemma's face got tighter and her eyes got bigger.

'I don't like it,' she said. I could see her eyes welling up.

'Neither do I,' I said. 'But there's no option. We need to know what we're dealing with, so I need to go and recce it. We're not just giving up, so we need to be ready to fight.'

Tears spilled down her cheeks and her chin trembled.

'Why us...this is shit.' She wiped her eyes with the back of her hand. 'This sucks. It's not enough to have a major disaster; we have to go and run-in with a bikie gang too, just to top off a really shitty situation.'

I couldn't argue that, so I stayed silent and let her vent. No matter which way I looked at it, there was no way around it. I had to try and corroborate what old Aroha had told us. If she was wrong, I'd be the happiest man alive. But if not, we needed to know and to be prepared.

'So what's the plan, then?' Gemma sniffed, took a breath and composed herself.

'Keep it simple,' I said. 'I go on my own on foot, sneak into the village for a recce, see what's going on, and bug out sharpish. Zip in, zip out.' I gave her a grin. 'Story of my life.'

She managed a smile.

'Not the best time for jokes, Mark,' she said. 'But I do love you.'

'Love you too.' I pulled her in and kissed the top of her head. 'It's gunna be okay.'

As I stroked her hair, I hoped I was right.

31

D awn had broken by the time Aroha reached the Maunsell property again.

She put Nellie away and stroked the animal's neck, gave her a pat on the flank and secured the gate again.

She knew she should be giving it a good brush but was dog-tired and just wanted to get home. Plus, she would have to go to the Maunsell's barn to fetch a brush and that would risk alerting someone to her presence, something she wanted to avoid.

As it turned out, she had no choice in the matter. Walking away from the gate, swinging the bit and reins gently in her hand, she spotted one of the Maunsell girls heading up the track towards her. She couldn't remember the girl's name, but she was the mouthy one of the family, the one who had got kicked out of school and did time in juvie.

Aroha noticed that the girl wore jeans and riding boots and had a bucket of feed in her hand.

The girl – Kym or Camryn or something like that, she thought – tossed her chin and called out.

'Hey Aroha, whatchu doin' so early?'

'Morning, dear.' Aroha smiled, playing the grandma bit. 'I just came to have a look at the horses. Reminds me of my childhood, riding the countryside all around here.' She smiled again, but the girl wasn't interested in stories of the olden days.

'How come you got that then?' She gestured towards the bit and reins in the old woman's hand.

'This?' Aroha looked at it as if just noticing it for the first time. 'Oh, I just brought them in case I thought I might have a ride.' She smiled widely. 'I think maybe riding might be a bit beyond me these days, dear. It's probably something best left for you young ones, I think.'

She chortled to herself, but noticed that the girl didn't join in.

'You din't ride one o' the horses, did you? You ain't s'posed to just come and use our shit.'

Aroha ignored the poor manners – manners she would've beaten out of the girl twenty years ago – and smiled again.

'No, no. But an old lady's allowed to dream, isn't she?' As soon as the lie left her lips she knew she'd slipped up, but it was already too late.

The girl scowled and started to move on.

'Just aks next time,' she grumbled. 'Ain't a charity.'

Aroha nodded and smiled and moved off in her own direction. The girl had known nothing but charity her whole life, having never held a job. And Aroha tut-tutted to herself over the girl's language.

'It's *ask*,' she muttered under her breath, 'not aks. An axe is for cutting wood.'

She didn't look back as she made her way home, but her heart was pounding in her chest. The girl wouldn't have to look too hard to realise one of the horses had been worked, no matter how gently, and then Aroha's lie would be revealed.

The Maunsells would be okay to deal with, and she was sure she could smooth things over with them. But if the word went around that Aroha had borrowed a horse overnight and things went wrong with the Bandits' planned attack, her situation could get dicey.

She would have to think of a cover for that and fast. But right now, she needed a cup of tea and some grass to calm her nerves.

Gazza nudged Mickey in the OP.

'Interesting,' he breathed.

Mickey flicked his eyebrows, not speaking. Something was up, but he couldn't quite peg what it was.

I HAD nothing concrete on which to trust the old woman, but my gut told me I should. She'd risked her life to come and warn us of the looming threat, which said a lot to me. It would've been easier for her just to sit back and play dumb – we were nothing to her, so why should she care if we lived or died?

I wasn't one to ponder too much, and right now I had more important things to do, like getting my shit together so I could get going.

I had the Bushmaster M4 plus five spare mags from Bevan's stash. The weapon would be either in my hands or hanging off me at all times, and the mags were handy in my belt pouches.

The Glock 17 was holstered on my right thigh and I had a spare mag for that too. The Ruger GP100 was holstered cross-draw on my left hip. It felt odd carrying two pistols and I'd be happy if I didn't need to use either of them, but it was better to be safe than sorry.

I had a Buck 692 Vanguard knife with a rubber grip sheathed on my left hip behind the Ruger. Even with a blade just over four inches, it was a tough, reliable hunting knife and was razor sharp. My other pouches carried a multi-tool, wound dressings, a bandanna and para cord – all items handy for many things. My daypack carried mostly extra medical supplies, water, 24-hours' worth of food, and extra ammo.

I was dressed lightly in cargo pants and a black T-shirt, and my boots were scuffed and comfortable.

'If I'm not back in five hours, you'll know something's wrong,' I told Gemma.

'Shouldn't take you that long, should it?' She crinkled up her nose like I'd farted.

'Hope not,' I said, 'but I can't just rock on down there and ask them what they're playing at, can I? I need to sneak in for a recce.'

'And sneak out again quick smart,' she told me firmly. 'Don't shag around trying to take them on. From what that woman said, they're ready for war.' She tugged at my sleeve. 'And we need you here in one piece.'

'I'll be sensible,' I said, trying to sound reassuring. I was pretty sure it didn't work. 'I'm not going to take on a bunch of savages with machine guns.'

A few more minutes to get myself sorted then she followed me out to the shed. The Honda Big Red quad bike had done many miles but was dependable and pretty good on gas. I had topped it up and had a spare tyre on the back, just in case.

I climbed aboard and kicked the engine over. It was reassuringly smooth. I gave Gemma a grin.

'See you shortly,' I said.

She leaned in and kissed me on the lips.

'Get in and get out,' she said. 'We need you back here.'

Archie and Jethro saw me off as I headed down the drive and I gave them a wave. It felt good to be on the quad with the wind in my face. Darren and his other son were at the roadblock and made room for me to get through. I pulled up beside them.

'Keep a close eye out,' I told them. 'I'll be back within five hours – hopefully these roosters aren't on the way already.'

'All good,' Darren said. He clapped me on the shoulder. 'Good luck.'

I motored on through and left the sanctity – however fragile – of our little community behind me as I headed towards Meremere.

Once I got to Mercer I avoided the expressway and stuck to the left, taking a narrow side road that wound its way up the hill to a handful of houses perched there. People were out working in their gardens or standing round talking and they all stopped to look as I went by, but no one approached me.

I gave them a friendly wave and kept going, having no interest in stopping. I also felt the pressure of time. Who knew how long we had? Who knew what would happen while I was gone? Bad things had a habit of happening, and I could only hope that this time would be different.

The side road came to a dead end but opening a gate allowed access into a farm track that ran off at an angle away from the expressway towards Meremere. It wasn't public land but the farm it crossed was run by the dairy company and this part of it was scrubby and largely disused. Weekend motocross riders used it for fun and burglars used it to get back home after hitting Mercer or dumping a stolen car.

I slowed up when I saw the village approaching, and steered the Honda off the track into a copse of trees. I killed the engine and listened to it ticking as it started to cool. After draping a camo-pattern tarpaulin over the quad, I added a few branches and used another branch to brush away my tyre-tracks from the dirt. With any luck the bike would be safe while I was gone.

I took a drink of water and checked my gear again, making sure I didn't rattle or squeak when I moved. Everything was good. I got the M4 in my hands, safety on, and set off. From here on in I needed to move tactically and take my time, watching all directions and making sure I didn't walk into a trap.

If the shit hit the fan I had no one to back me up, so I would need to shoot and scoot. It wasn't a comfortable feeling, but that's how it was.

I just had to crack on and get it done.

32

The shrieks got louder as Sandy hurried across the paddock. She'd heard the first one from the washing line and thought at first it was a cat fight. As she reached the gully, it became clear it was anything but.

Through the trees and undergrowth she could see people moving on the far side, on the edge of Clyde and Ellette's property. She couldn't tell who it was, but they were moving quickly towards the road and she could hear angry voices.

Sandy moved parallel to them, glancing over her shoulder to the house. Nobody else was in sight and she suddenly felt very exposed. The washing was rippling gently on the washing line. She could hear the faint hum of the generator in the distance.

She reached the boundary fence at the roadside, a low ditch between it and the asphalt. Three people were coming along the road towards her now; a man, a woman and a little girl. The man was hunched over and holding his face, blood running between his fingers. He was moaning and muttering to himself, and the woman had her hand on his arm to guide him. The girl saw Sandy first and alerted the adults.

The woman fixed on her and immediately started swearing, jabbing a finger in Sandy's direction.

'You coulda fuckin' killed him! He's blinded now 'cause of you and that prick, you ripped his fuckin' face open!'

Sandy took an involuntary step backwards at the vitriol. The woman was so wound up that dry spit was flying from her lips.

'Where is that prick? I'll fuckin' kill him! He tried to kill us – he could've killed my baby.'

The little girl was staring at Sandy with an unnervingly blank expression. Sandy guessed she and the woman were the ones that Mark had run off earlier. They were only a few metres away now, stopped in the road so the woman could unleash her fury. Sandy could see the man was bleeding quite heavily, streams of red running down his forearms and onto his clothes.

He lifted his hands away enough to look at her, and she could see an open wound in his cheek near his eye. It was leaking dark blood.

'Fuck you,' the man hissed at her.

The sight of the wound and the hatred coming from them had Sandy's heart thumping and she felt her knees wobble beneath her.

'I think you should go,' she managed to get out, before the woman cut her off.

'You go get that prick, get him out here and see what he's done. He tried to kill my baby and I'm gunna kill him myself.'

Sandy saw the woman's gaze shift behind her, and her expression changed.

'Oh, here we go,' she scoffed. 'More bully-boys, come to have a go too, have ya?'

Sandy heard her daughter's voice behind her.

'Get lost,' Gemma snarled, sounding harder than Sandy had ever heard her. 'Don't you come round here and threaten us, you loser.'

The woman sneered at her as Gemma came level with Sandy. 'Or what?'

'Or you'll come off second best,' Rob said, joining them.

'Fuck you, old man,' the man growled, raising an eye to scowl at them.

'No,' Rob said, drawing the Browning and holding it by his side. 'Actually, fuck you.' He eyeballed the pair of them, ignoring the little girl. 'Now get moving before I get grumpy.'

They held their position for a long moment but he didn't flinch. Gemma had the M3 sub machine gun in her hands and lifted it to her shoulder.

'Think we're scared of you?' the woman said, giving a weak sneer that belied the truth. 'We'll be back, and we got guns and shit too. You'll be sorry, arseholes.'

'Get going,' Rob said coldly.

They shuffled off, waiting until they were twenty metres down the road before throwing more colourful threats back at the family. They crossed the road and cut across a paddock near the Van Dijk's place, heading away towards the next road over, where Rusty had indicated they may be living.

'We need to watch them,' Rob said, keeping an eye on them until they were out of sight.

Gemma took her mother's arm and guided her back towards the house. 'You okay, Mum?'

Sandy nodded weakly. 'I could have done without that.'

'Must've walked into one of the booby-traps,' Rob said behind them. 'That was a nasty looking wound.'

'Shouldn't have come stealing then,' Gemma said bluntly. 'It wouldn't have happened if they hadn't come on our property.'

Sandy glanced her, unsettled by the hardness her daughter was showing. She kept her thoughts to herself for now.

Rob turned and looked behind them. He could see Clyde watching them from his property, making no attempt to hide himself.

'And as for that dickhead,' Rob muttered, 'he's trouble, too.'

Hearing the door to the mobile home open, Blake cracked an eye open and half sat up on the bed. Expecting to see Archie coming to visit – and probably wanting to play – he was surprised to see a different visitor.

'Jenny,' he said, propping himself up on his elbow. He yawned and pushed up into a sitting position. The blanket covering him fell away. 'Hi.'

'Oh good,' she said, stepping up into the doorway. 'You're awake.'

Still waking up, he wasn't sure whether that was sarcasm in her voice or not, but it sounded pretty close.

'Is it time to change the dressing?' he said. He swung his legs to the floor and pulled back the sleeve of his T-shirt to check his wound. The shoulder was stiff and sore but the dressing hadn't leaked through.

'No, I haven't come for that,' she said, and he could tell now from her tone that she was pissed.

'Okay,' he said carefully, his mind starting to tick over as he wondered what he'd done to piss her off. 'What's up?'

Jenny folded her arms across her chest and gave him a hard stare.

'You need to get up and get busy,' she said abruptly. 'There's no time for you to be loafing about in here.'

Blake's eyebrows shot up in surprise; he hadn't seen that coming. The look on the older woman's face told him she wasn't kidding.

'Okay,' he repeated. 'Have I done something...'

'No,' she said irritably, 'and that's the problem. Everyone else's too polite to tell you, but I'm telling you. We've got our hands full here, and Mark's gone off to find out whether we're about to be attacked. Meanwhile,' and she gestured at him sitting on the bed, 'you're having a snooze and being looked after.'

Blake bristled. 'To be fair, I did get shot,' he said. 'I haven't slept properly in days and I...you know...I was out there, patrolling and what not...'

'Yes, I know you got shot, because I've been looking after you,' Jenny snapped back. 'And none of us have slept properly, so you're not alone there either. But we need all hands to the pump, and you could do more to earn your keep, don't you think?'

'Earn my keep?' He gave her the look he reserved for juvenile offenders who gave him attitude. 'Sorry, I didn't realise it was like that.'

Jenny pursed her lips and gave him a withering glare.

'We all have to pitch in and do our bit,' she said firmly. 'No one expects you to be doing heavy lifting, but there's plenty you can do, and it shouldn't all fall on the shoulders of the older generation here.'

The force of her personality was palpable, and Blake could see he wasn't going to win this argument any time soon. He sighed and got to his feet. He gave his wounded shoulder a rub and looked at her.

'I didn't mean to get offside with you, Jenny,' he said quietly. 'And I fully appreciate everything you guys have done so far for me.'

He waited and she gave a small nod.

'What can I do to help?'

'Follow me.'

She led the way to the sleepout, where they found Rob sorting an array of weapons laid out on the floor He looked up as they stepped into the room. He ran an appraising eye over Blake.

'Good to see you're up,' he said, and Blake felt his cheeks flush. 'You any good with these?'

Blake glanced at the guns. 'M4 and Glock, obviously,' he said. 'I've done a bit of shooting, so most of them I should be okay with. Never fired a machine gun, though.'

'It's not full automatic,' Rob said, 'so it's just a big rifle, really. Are you able to load and reload?'

Blake picked up the Bushmaster M4 and awkwardly slung it. Using the far wall as his safe direction, he managed to drop the magazine but couldn't reinsert it using his left hand. He grimaced with the pain of working that shoulder, and Rob shook his head.

'That's no good then,' he said. 'No help if you can't reload.'

'What about if someone helped me?'

The older man looked at him curiously as he took the M4 back.

'What, you mean like a spotter?'

'Sort of. If I had two guns, I could use one and swap it with them when I'm out of ammo, then they can reload it and swap back again.'

Rob gave an approving look. 'That could work. It'd have to be one of the ladies, though. And you'd need magazine-fed weapons only.' He glanced to Jenny, who was listening silently. 'What d'you think, Jenny?'

'Yep,' she said cautiously, tossing the idea around. 'That could probably work.'

She nodded to herself, realising the idea made sense. Blake had the training and skills to be used as a shooter; he just needed some help to do it. She looked up, realising that Rob was still watching her. He had a questioning look on his face.

'What?' Jenny said. 'Ohhh...right.' She turned to Blake, then back to Rob. 'I see.'

'That's decided then.' Rob laid the M4 back in place. 'You can use that and the .22, unless you want to use a shotgun.'

'Might be a bit too much kick for me just yet,' Blake said. 'A .22's easy.

'Okay, I'll use the BAR. Gemma and Alex have got theirs.'

Blake touched his shoulder again, massaging it gently with his fingertips. 'Kinda feel like we're preparing for war,' he said.

Rob looked at him sharply. 'That's exactly what we're doing,' he said firmly. 'And you better be ready for it.'

33

The track looped back on itself and I moved past it into a gully that I knew would take me to the edge of the village. The vegetation was undisturbed and it didn't look like anyone had been down there in a while. As it got close to the end I saw more signs of activity – discarded beer and pre-mixed bourbon cans, cheap chip packets and cigarette butts. A pair of underwear mashed into the dirt told another story and I could only imagine the unnatural deeds that had taken place down here.

I moved slowly to the lip of the gully, taking my time to stop, listen and look. I could hear activity in the distance but it was impossible to tell exactly where, and it was just indiscriminate noise. The only things I could make out were snatches of music – some kind of bass – and the odd bang like a door slamming.

I crouched in the undergrowth at the edge of the gully for a good couple of minutes, taking stock of my surroundings. Straight ahead of me was waste ground where the town had stopped growing. Overgrown with weeds, a pair of abandoned cars that had been there so long weeds were growing up through them, and another one that had been burned out and left.

That one was recent, the ground around it scorched in a wide circle, and the smell of burnt rubber and oil still obvious. Maybe a few days ago, just before the national emergency was declared. A sign of what I could expect from the town, in case I'd had any doubts.

The waste ground was about the size of a couple of rugby fields and ran in both directions, disappearing into trees to my left and hitting a minor road to my right. Corrugated iron fences straight ahead, the back boundary of a street. Cookie-cutter state houses beyond the fences; tiled roofs, brickwork and single tin garages.

I did a quick check of my gear to make sure I hadn't lost anything, plotted out my next move, and took a deep breath.

Running bent over, I made it to the first car wreck and paused, re-checking. No sign that I'd been detected. No dogs barking. No shots or shouts.

Lifting my feet so I didn't trip on unseen hazards in the weeds, I raced across to the fence, crouched with my back to it, and scanned behind me. Nothing, nobody. So far, so good.

I tracked along the fence line, keeping a couple of metres from it to avoid bumping into the tin and causing a racket. I had no doubt at all what kind of reception I could expect if I got sprung.

I passed the back of several houses before reaching the end of the fence, and took a knee there, my mouth half open, eyes scanning. I checked my back first – no point moving ahead if someone was creeping up behind.

All clear.

I was unaware of the hidden eyes watching me.

The trees that ended the stretch of waste ground curved round to my right, out of sight, and in my mind's eye I plotted where that cover would take me. Close to the school, which was off the main drag.

I got down on my belly and edged up to the corner, keeping as flat as I could, the M4 in one hand. Peering cautiously around the corner, I saw that the waste ground continued up to the road, the open ground being the width of a couple of properties. Houses that had never been built in a town that never took off. The weeds here were lower, as if the section was used to play on by local kids. Or, judging by the discarded crap and skid marks from motorbikes, maybe older kids.

The street I was looking at was a residential side street. There was a car up on blocks on the other side. A pair of sneakers hung over the power line, indicating the presence of a tinnie house.

The windows in the houses across the road had a good view of the waste ground, but even with my small binoculars, I couldn't see anyone. I had two options if I was going to continue on from here; carry on straight ahead, being as tactical as I could, or divert over to the cover of the trees. Using the trees would take more time, and it was something I didn't have a lot of. I debated for a minute, weighing up speed against caution, and common sense won out. I backed over to the trees, entered the shade and went right, keeping several metres inside the cover as I made my way past the waste ground. As I moved, carefully placing my feet, I kept a constant eye out for traps, people and dogs.

I made my way through the trees and undergrowth until I could see the playing fields of the school to my right. The cover thinned out there too, and I dropped to a knee, scanning ahead. The school looked untouched, all closed up and no one about. Beyond it was the main drag with the community hall down to the left. Houses were on both sides and across the road from the school.

Based on my previous visit, the hall was the seat of activity in the village so that was what I wanted to see. I worked out angles, checked my gear again, and moved off. Using the school buildings as cover, I made my way along the boundary fence into the school grounds, keeping low and moving steadily. Move too fast and you stand out – better to be steady and ready.

I got to a classroom and took a knee behind it, catching my breath and scanning again. I was sweaty and dirty, but my focus was on getting a good look at what was happening in the village so I could plan ahead. I cocked an ear, not sure whether I had heard something or not. A door slammed somewhere and I heard a dog howl.

I took a breath, got to my feet, and peeked around the corner of the building.

Clear.

I plotted my next move, came around the corner of the building and moved soundlessly to the next corner, the M4 in the shoulder and my thumb on the safety, ready to rock'n'roll.

I got to the next corner.

DION AND PUA watched the commando sneaking through the school.

They'd been tracking him as he made his way through the bush, once he'd caught the eye of one of the kids. The kid was a glue-head and used one of the dumped cars in the wasteland as his hidey-hole. Usually neither of the big brothers would have any time for him, but today he'd done good. Real good.

With his Steyr at the ready, Pua led the way around the front of the school, moving surprisingly fast for such a big man. Dion covered his back in case there was more than one. They had no idea who he was, but whoever he was, he was in for a treat today. Meremere was their base for as long as LD said it was, and they would defend it to the bitter end.

They reached the school hall and stopped, listening. Pua looked to Dion and pointed up and over, indicating the commando was on the other side of the building. Dion had no clue how his brother knew shit like that, it was like the guy was telepathic.

He'd always been a sneaky bastard though. Back in Oz there'd been a series of intruder rapes over several years in and around the area Pua had lived. It was big news and the cops had a task force and everything, but they never caught the guy. Dion had always suspected it was his brother, but he never had the balls to challenge him.

Pua was a scary motherfucker on a good day.

Dion nodded and started to move to the right, but was stopped by a big mitt on his arm. Pua put a finger to his lips and pointed again.

The commando was coming.

I MOVED CAREFULLY along the side of the hall, M4 up and eyes everywhere.

Adrenaline was pumping and sweat was running down my chest. Once I got to the corner, I took a knee and scanned. The school yard was empty but my senses were pinging. I could feel the threat in the air – this was a dangerous place to be. Not far to go now and I'd be close enough for a decent look at what was going on, then I could bug out and get home, back to relative safety.

It would have made more sense to have a buddy alongside me on a recce like this but I didn't have one, so had to make do.

I took a breath, scanned, and edged to the corner. Everywhere I looked, so did the muzzle of the M4. The idea was to keep my weapon back from the corner itself, checking first so I didn't bumble around into the unknown.

I took a first peek, seeing concrete with tiger turf beyond it, and edged out slightly further, quartering the unseen area bit by bit. A trickle of sweat was tickling me between my shoulder blades.

The tiniest sound behind me sent my senses screaming and I snapped my head around, moving to get my weapon round too. There was a big man, very big, a few metres behind me, pointing a Steyr at me. If he fired at this range I was toast, and we both knew it.

At the same time as this thought was hitting the front of my brain, another huge guy appeared from my left, coming around the corner I'd just been quartering. He seized hold of my left bicep with a hand bigger than my head, wrenched me off-balance, and went for the Bushmaster.

With him now so close, I knew the other guy was less likely to shoot, so I took my chances. I twisted, pulling against the guy's grip, but it was like my arm was jammed in a bank vault door. It was going numb from the pressure of his grip and he was still yanking at me, not letting me get any stability or momentum.

He was a big ugly sucker and somewhere in the back of my head I recognised his mug, probably from an intelligence notice back in the day. I certainly recognised his type and the Bandits patch he wore.

I could hear the other guy shouting but I was too focussed on the second guy to listen. I managed to keep the M4 from his reach but it also prevented me from getting it on line to take him out. I dropped it on its sling and went for the holstered Glock instead. He saw what I was doing and lunged at me, swiping at my right hand with his other huge mitt. The other guy was going mental too, but in all the confusion I got the Glock out and was just starting to lift the barrel when I got hit by a freight train from behind and went flying. I managed to keep hold of the Glock but someone also managed to get hold of the M4 sling, and as my legs flew up in the air and my body gained momentum, I was hit across the throat by the sling.

It stopped me dead in mid-air and my legs swung forward under me like a pendulum. My head was getting ripped off at the same time and a second later I hit the concrete flat on my back, the wind exploding from my lungs. The back of my head hit the ground too and bright confetti burst across my vision.

I gaped like a fish out of water, my squashed lungs desperate to get some air, but without success before the first boot slammed into my side. I grunted and gasped and tried to roll away but the monster on the other side returned the favour and sent me back the way I'd come. A boot stamped down on my gun hand and ground it into the concrete, forcing the Glock from my grasp, as if I even had the ability to do anything with it just now.

With my whole torso locked up tight as a drum and wheezing for oxygen, I stared into the barrels of twin assault rifles. Behind them the sun was blocked out by two massive men, eyeing me with relish.

'You fucked, bro,' one of them grinned.

I couldn't have agreed more.

34

The pig watched him with sleepy eyes as Blake leaned on the fence railing. It was a typical kunekune – short and fat, with a hairy black and white coat.

Blake reached over and patted the pig on the head. It snorted and snuffled at his hand, seeking food. It was well-tamed and obviously well-fed.

The wound pulled when he stretched down, and Blake felt a sharp jolt of pain. He winced and pulled back, putting a hand to it gingerly. He knew he should have been resting, but he had the feeling it wouldn't be looked on favourably.

They were a funny bunch, he'd decided. Mark was the exact opposite of him in a work sense – Blake knew he wouldn't have liked working with him. He was all aggression and organisation, constantly on the move, prepared to take anything on. Blake preferred a slower pace of life and let things come to him, rather than chasing anything too hard.

His wife, Gemma, was a funny one. On the face of it she was a normal wife and mother, caring and nurturing, but beneath that façade was something tougher. He'd heard something of her experiences the last few days with Alex, and it was clear she was not a lady to be messed with. She had made him feel welcome though, and for that he was grateful.

He heard the crunch of feet on the gravel and turned. Rob was coming towards him from the sleepout. The old man was another one; a tough old rooster, but a real softie at heart.

'What're you doing?' Rob's tone was neutral but for some reason it made Blake wary.

'Just getting some fresh air,' he said, pushing up from the fence. He tried a smile. Rob stopped a few feet away and glanced at the pig then back to Blake. He wasn't smiling in return.

'All rested up? How's the arm?'

'Not bad.' Blake touched it instinctively. It throbbed and he was due for more painkillers. Unfortunately they didn't have anything hospital-grade, so the throbbing was a constant companion.

'Good.' Rob gave a short nod. 'I'll probably find you something to do before long.'

Blake did a mental double-take, unsure if the older man was winding him up or not. When their eyes met, Blake knew he wasn't.

'No time for lazing around,' Rob said brusquely, hooking his thumbs in the front belt loops of his jeans. 'Even if you're wounded. Best thing you can do is get up and crack on, not sit around commiserating with yourself.'

'I haven't exactly been commiserating with myself,' Blake said, feeling obliged to defend himself. Jesus, the older folk were riding his arse all of a sudden and he didn't know why.

'Look, sunshine,' he said, 'I've known plenty of servicemen in my time. I was in the Navy, see? I've known a lot of very tough buggers, very hard men. The sort of men you knew, you just knew, you could rely on them. Come hell or high water, you could rely on them.' He looked Blake in the eye, and Blake could see the underlying hardness there. 'I have to say; you're not one of them.'

Blake recoiled from the blunt assessment and opened his mouth to protest, but Rob cut him off with a warning finger.

'I don't mean that as a criticism.'

'Well it's hardly a compliment,' Blake said.

Rob shrugged. 'No, not really. It wasn't meant to be, either. But what I'm saying to you is, you need to step up. Wounded or not, you're expected to step up and pull your weight, see?'

Blake decided it was probably best to just listen for now.

'We're all in this together,' Rob continued, his tone softening ever so slightly, 'and I know you had some hard times out there. Having your mate killed can't have been easy.'

Blake nodded, the loss of Luke another constant companion. The emotions came in waves, sometimes surprising him in their ferocity.

'What I'm saying to you, John,' Rob told him, 'is that we're more than happy to have you here and help out. And I know Jenny's already had a word, as she does.' He gave the hint of a wry smile. 'There's a lot of respect in our family for Police and the like. But.' He looked Blake hard in the eye. 'But you can't afford to be feeling sorry for yourself, either. You need to be on your game, see?'

Blake nodded again, absorbing the speech. He didn't know how to respond, so he simply stuck out his hand. Rob shook it firmly.

'Fair enough,' he said.

'Good,' Rob said. 'Now come with me. We've got work to do.'

35

My captors led me to the community hall at gunpoint, one behind me, one to the side. They'd stripped me of my weapons and my hands were on my head, fingers interlocked. My body ached but my mind was racing.

When the "501" deportees had started being sent over from Australia, a swathe of intelligence had come with them. They were some of the worst criminals in Aussie, and unfortunately, they were all born in New Zealand. Didn't matter that most of them had no other connection to this country, had lived their whole lives over the ditch and all their families and roots were there.

The Aussie government decreed that they were Kiwis, not worthy of living in the land of endless sunshine, bad beer and sheilas, and would be sent "home". I admired that about the Aussies – they knew it wasn't popular with their Kiwi counterparts but they didn't give a shit, because it was best for their own country.

Many of the 501s were members of outlaw motorcycle gangs and they were experts in their field. They gave the ethnic gangs here a lesson in organised crime and everyone lifted their game, but the deportees ran the show. They were a breed apart and they changed the face of the criminal underworld here.

The Bandits were one of the worst gangs we were given.

And here I was, captured at gunpoint by two of them and being walked into the hornets' nest.

It wasn't quite how I'd planned this quick recce, and I was wishing like hell that I'd just played it safe and stayed away.

The hall was dead ahead now and the crowd outside didn't look inviting. At least a dozen were patched-up Bandits, and a row of hogs was lined up outside. There were Steyrs, tats and patches everywhere.

Too late to worry about it now; I had to play it as it came.

A man stepped out of the hall, shades doing nothing to hide his staunch look. I recognised him immediately. I couldn't recall his real name straight away, but I knew him by his reputation and his nickname – Little Dog.

He was the Sergeant-at-Arms for the Bandits last I heard, but as he came closer I saw the President's badge on the front of his patch vest. Moving up in the world. I doubted his reputation had changed with his office; he was a bad bastard through and through. Behind him came another guy I recognised. The guy I had butted heads with when Bevan and I visited this shithole of a town. We had come with the intention of ending their feud with us once and for all, but things hadn't quite panned out that way.

They made way to us, Little Dog looking staunch, the other guy letting a slight smirk show on his ugly mug.

The rest of the crowd had gathered around in a semi-circle, eager to see the prisoner and no doubt wanting some action.

'Who the fuck is this?' Little Dog growled, eyeing me from behind his shades.

'Caught him sneaking in through the school,' one of the big apes behind me said. 'Had this.'

He handed my M4 to Little Dog, who looked first at it then at me. 'You a cop.'

It wasn't a question, but I shook anyway.

'Na.'

He scowled at me, taking my gun belt from one of his boys.

'Carrying cop guns,' he said. 'Look like a cop.'

The other guy behind him interjected.

'He's the one came here before,' he said. 'He's the one shot up Henry an' them. Come an' took our guns.'

I didn't point out that it was only one gun; it probably wasn't the best time. I focussed instead on how the fuck I was going to get out of this. Force seemed an unlikely option, so did negotiation – bluff or sleight of hand were probably the most likely options available.

'I'm not a cop,' I said, trying to keep my voice calm and non-confrontational. These guys held all the cards – challenging them would only bring me pain.

'Bullshit,' the second guy said. He sidled up beside Little Dog, eyeballing me. 'I can smell the fuckin' bacon on you, boy. You're full o' shit. Whatchu come here for anyway? You come here all gunned up – whatchu come for?'

'I'm not a cop,' I repeated. 'I came here chasing someone, I thought he came from here.'

'Bullshit,' the guy repeated. I could see the Sergeant-at-Arms badge on his chest. I didn't know who he was, but he was a man to watch.

'It's true. He came and fired some shots at us and took off, I figured he was one of your guys. I chased him through Mercer and lost him. He was headed this way on foot.'

I knew it was weak but it was the best I could do on the spot, so I had to press on and stick to it.

'I lost him in the gully just over the back there,' I said, focussing on Little Dog. I couldn't see his eyes but I knew he was listening. 'I came up into the school to see if I could find him. I was about to give up and go when your dudes jumped me.'

Little Dog looked past me to the two big fellas.

'Where'd you find him?'

'In the school,' one of them said.

'Eh...' He looked back at me and pursed his lips thoughtfully. 'On 'is own, eh?'

'Yeah.'

'I don't know where the guy went,' I said, 'I lost him in the gully and he was a good couple of hundred metres ahead of me. He may have gone right past, or got into town before these guys saw me.'

'Full o' shit,' the second guy growled. 'He's fuckin' lyin', Dog.' He scowled at me. 'Why the fuck else you come here all gunned up, 'less you come to attack us?'

'Why would I come to attack you?' I said. Talking was good – while we were talking, they weren't killing me. I was good to talk all day. 'I'm one guy against all you; it'd be suicide to try that. These guys caught me and I hadn't even fired a shot. Look, I'm not a soldier and I'm not a cop. I'm just a guy who's fuckin' sick of people stealing my shit and shooting at my family.'

Little Dog and the other guy looked at each other.

'Whaddaya think, Jake?' Little Dog said.

Jake scowled harder. 'He killed Henry an' them, come and threatened us, then comes back to have a go.' He turned his gaze back to me. 'Kill 'im.'

Little Dog pursed his lips again, and I could see he was thinking hard. That was good. Jake had put him on the spot though, which wasn't good. The President would never want to look weak, especially when his enforcer wanted to follow a course of action that would make him look strong. Brutality was key with these guys. It all depended on whether Little Dog had the balls to make his own mind up or not.

Little Dog turned his attention to me again.

'You a farmer?'

'No.' I shook my head.

Little Dog looked to Jake. 'I thought you said they went to a farm?'

Jake tossed his chin. 'Did.'

Little Dog paused and an unspoken message passed between them. I saw it coming but could do nothing to stop it.

Jake took two fast steps forward and threw a jab into my face. I managed to pull my head back fractionally and avoid some of the force, but it still hit like a runaway tank and knocked me backwards into one of the big fellas. I didn't have to pretend too hard that it hurt and I was disoriented. The big unit behind me pushed me forward and I staggered, trying to clear my head and hoping another tank wasn't coming.

'He's on a farm,' Jake said. 'Cyrus told me; he's been there.'

'So he got food and animals and shit,' Little Dog said. 'Shit we can use.'

'Aye.'

Through the spinning in my head I managed to follow what they were saying. It wasn't good.

'No...' I shook my head and got myself straight. I sucked in a breath 'We got robbed. That's what I'm saying. We've got nothing because we keep getting robbed.'

The two gangsters eyed me and I knew they didn't believe me. I had no option but to push on.

'I thought you guys had taken our animals.' I held my hands up in surrender. 'We've run out of food, man. We've got nothing. I haven't eaten since yesterday.'

Little Dog looked to Jake then back at me. 'Tough shit,' he said. 'Get some boys round there, Jake. Keep this cunt here 'til it's done, then kill him.'

With that the President turned and headed back inside the hall.

Jake fixed me with a nasty grin. 'This is gunna be fun,' he smirked.

36

R ob and Sandy had loaded up a wheelbarrow with food, and Archie put a couple more boxes in his own wagon. They walked together down the driveway and across the road.

Rob had told the other neighbours to come down earlier, when he took Blake around to meet them all. A decent portion of the scavenged supplies had been put aside to share out amongst the neighbours. Mark had taken some gentle persuasion from Gemma to agree to it, but he knew the benefit of paying it forward. It was no secret that they'd secured some extra supplies, and there was no point getting offside for the sake of a few meals.

Even Clyde and Ellette had come over to pick some up. Rob had been amused that they were wary about running into Mark, only relaxing when they realised he wasn't home. It had still stuck in his craw that they'd had the cheek to come over though.

Sophie greeted them at the door with a big smile. She waved them in and tried for a hug from Archie, but he dodged away and carried a box of cereal inside.

Sandy laughed. 'Good luck getting a hug out of him,' she said. 'Even Nana has to be patient.'

Sophie smiled. 'He'sh a good boy. Come in, come in,' she said, 'Rushty ish jusht having a resht.'

Rob noticed that, despite the smile, her eyes were not twinkling as they normally did. He could see the strain in her face and the tension in her shoulders. He guessed they were all feeling it, and wondered how he looked to everyone else. He followed his wife and grandson inside, carrying an armful of supplies.

Placing the box of tinned fruit and vegetables on the bench, he looked over to where Rusty was asleep in his armchair. He hadn't stirred since they had entered the house.

Sophie gazed at him softly. 'He ish very tired,' she said apologetically. 'That attack really took it out of him, poor dear.'

Sandy put her arm around the other woman's shoulders and gave her a squeeze.

'I'm not surprised,' she said, 'he was a lucky man.' She gave a reassuring smile. 'He'll be okay, Sophie. He just needs to rest up and he'll bounce right back.'

Sophie caught her breath and managed a smile.

'Of coursh he will,' she said, wiping her eyes before clasping her hands together. 'Of coursh he will.'

Rob shifted his feet uncomfortably. Emotional times like this were Sandy's domain, not his. He was surprised when Archie left his side and went to the older Dutch woman, wrapping his arms around her waist. He gave her a tight squeeze.

'It'll be okay, Sophie,' he told her. 'Rusty just needs some sleep and he'll be fine. And chicken soup.'

She leaned down to him and returned the hug, tears brimming as she kissed the top of his head.

Archie pulled away and looked up at her. 'Chicken soup always makes you feel better when you're sick,' he said. 'Mum always says that, anyway. I don't like chicken soup though, myself.'

Sophie patted his cheek and wiped her eyes again, and Rob gave his wife the signal to get moving. They left the Van Dijks and headed down to the roadblock, where Sean and his wife were taking a stint.

Having missed out earlier, they gratefully accepted a delivery of food and were keen to chat. While Rob was chatting to Sean, he felt a tug at his sleeve.

'Poppa,' Archie was saying. 'There's strangers down the road.'

Rob spotted a pair of adults coming onto the road from Clyde and Ellette's driveway. They were both carrying items in their arms.

'Who is it, Poppa?'

'I don't know, buddy.' Rob turned to Sean with his hand out. 'Pass me those binoculars, Sean.'

He focussed in on the couple, identifying a teenage boy and girl. They were scruffy looking and he had never seen them before. He recognised a box the girl was carrying as one that Clyde had picked up from them earlier. He passed the bino's back to Sean, who also took a look.

'They live around here?' he said.

'Never seen them before,' Sean said. 'They don't live around here. Now they're climbing the fence into Darren's paddock.'

Rob frowned, his sixth sense pinging. 'I bet you they're from that group that've been round begging and stealing. We ran some of them off earlier.'

'I think it is them, Poppa,' Archie piped up. He was stroking his chin thoughtfully. 'I think they're the same family.'

Rob raised an eyebrow. 'Yeah? What makes you say that?'

'They've got the same colour hair.'

Sean grinned at Rob over the boy's head. 'Fair enough.'

'I think you're right, little man,' Rob said. 'I'm going to see where they go.'

The two women had stopped talking to listen, and Sandy put a hand on his arm.

'You're not going off chasing kids,' she told him firmly. 'That's just ridiculous.'

They both knew what she really meant, and Rob frowned some more, readying himself to argue the point. The look in his wife's eyes stopped him, and he relented.

'I'll go,' Sean said quickly. 'I'll track them from Rusty's place.'

He hurried off before anyone could argue, jogging down the road to the Van Dijk's gate and into their property. They saw him fence hopping a few paddocks away from the two teenagers, who were ducking in and out of sight behind hedges as they headed towards the next road over.

Ten minutes later he was back, panting and sweaty-faced from the unexpected exertion.

'They went to a house over on the next road,' he reported. 'I don't think they saw me.' He wiped his face on his sleeve and took a drink his wife handed him. 'I saw that woman there, the one that came round begging with the little girl. Looks like they live there.'

'I knew it,' Archie said, giving a fist pump and looking to his granddad for approval.

Rob ruffled the boy's hair and nodded.

'They're trouble,' he said, 'but now we know where they live, we need to keep an eye on them.'

'It'd be good if the others didn't encourage them,' Sandy said, and Rob grunted.

'They're idiots,' he said. 'We can't trust them. As soon as Mark gets back, we need to make a plan to deal with them.'

'Which ones?' Sean asked.

Rob set his jaw. 'All of them,' he said.

37

L ittle Dog fired up a smoke and took a long, slow drag.

He held it in, savouring the nicotine hit as he watched one of the boys walking up the road towards him. It was one of the boys they'd liberated from the prison – what a fuckin' rush that had been – and he had a chick in tow. Some young thing, kinda skanky looking but not the ugliest bit he'd seen in this shithole little town.

Sooner they got outta here the better. Little Dog was not a Mere-mere kinda dude.

The guy left the chick at the roadside and approached Little Dog at the entrance to the hall.

'Yo.'

'Who's it, my bro?' Little Dog took another draw on his smoke and waited.

'Chick's called Camreen,' the gangster said, jerking a thumb over his shoulder. 'Lives just outta town on a farm. Says she got some information for you.'

Little Dog sniffed and flicked his eyebrows. He looked past his boy to where the girl waited, arms folded and looking round at the gangsters hanging about. She had gumboots and dirty jeans and a stained blue singlet that showed off a large tat on her shoulder.

She saw him looking and stared back. Not afraid. *Girl's got sass.*

'Yeah, 'bout what?'

The guy looked away. 'Dunno, LD. Won't tell me. Says she only talk to the dog, yo.'

Little Dog felt a smile tug at his lips. Girl got sass, alright. Took balls say that to a Bandit. He tossed his chin towards the girl and waved her forward. 'Yo.'

She came over and Little Dog waved the guy away. He eyed the girl. She was skanky alright, with that wiggle to her ass when she moved and that purple bra peeking out under the singlet. Play her cards right, she get a ride alright.

'Camleen?' he said. 'Kinda name that, girl?'

She gave a sulky look as if she was annoyed. 'Dunno,' she said. 'What it is.'

Little Dog eyed her hard. 'Talkin' to the dog, bitch. Show some fuckin' respect.'

That got her right, and she picked up her lip.

'Shit, s'posed to be Carleen,' she said. 'Old man was pissed when he done it, wrote it wrong on the paper.'

Little Dog laughed, the story so goddamn stupid it had to be true. Even the girl managed to chuckle a little.

'That's some dumb shit,' he said. He offered her a smoke and she took it, holding it while he lit it with an engraved Zippo. Little Dog liked his Zippo – it was another status symbol that told people he was someone.

'Thanks.' She took a drag and cocked her head back, blowing the smoke over her shoulder.

Little Dog grinned to himself at the cheap move. Girl was good to go. He reminded himself she had come to see him about more than just putting it out there.

'You wanna talk to me?' he said.

She nodded and took another drag. He noticed her hand was trembling ever so slightly.

'Got a snitch,' she said. 'Ol' lady...took our horse last night. Dunno where she went, but she bullshit me 'bout it when she come back.'

Little Dog listened, flicking his ciggie butt aside.

'Reckon she done something she shouldn'ta,' Camleen went on. She sucked on the smoke, the tip glowing fierce orange and black. 'Maybe went and talked to that guy.'

Her eyes flicked up to Little Dog's. 'I know you got him here an' all, but funny he turn up after she gone all night, don'tcha think?'

Damn right it was funny. He knew that prick was lying. He whistled to the gangster who'd brough the girl to him.

'Get Jake,' he said.

He turned back to the girl as the gangster hustled off.

'Done good, girl,' he said, and he saw a flush of pleasure cross her face. 'All goods? Home all goods?'

She nodded and stubbed out her smoke. 'Yeah, thanks. All goods.'

Little Dog reached out and touched her face, sliding his hand down her smooth cheek. She didn't flinch.

'Got enough food and all that?'

'Yeah.' She nodded, maybe even pressing her cheek against his palm a little.

Jake jogged up and Little Dog gave him a toss of the chin.

''sup, Dog?'

'Girl come see me,' Little Dog said. 'Got a snitch, gone and seen that guy, the spy.'

Jake scowled. There was only way a snitch got dealt with, and as the Sgt-at-Arms the responsibility fell to him. He looked from Little Dog to the girl – one of the Maunsell girls, he realised now.

'Who's it?' he growled. 'Who's the snitch?'

Camleen had grown up round here, and she knew who Jake was. She also knew who his family were. She looked him in the eye.

'Aroha,' she said.

38

T he work that Rob had referred to wasn't quite what Blake had imagined. After the verbal serve that he'd been given, he was expecting some sort of beasting.

Instead, he was taken to the roadblock to meet whoever was on guard at the moment – Brenton was there with one of the farmhands from the Macklin farm, a young guy named Caleb.

Rob made the introductions and Blake shook hands with the two men. After checking everything was okay and confirming who was replacing them on watch, Rob walked him down the road, past Bevan's place then the Van Dijk's, and on to Darren's. Half an hour was spent meeting him and his family, followed by Brenton's wife Linda and the kids.

Farewelling them and heading towards the next place, Blake gestured back towards Linda's house.

'Was that a sawn-off shotgun I saw by the door there?' he said.

Rob glanced at him sideways. 'Probably,' he said.

Blake raised his eyebrows but said nothing, figuring it was best to keep his thoughts to himself.

'Mark gave it to them,' Rob told him. 'Took it off a bad guy.'

'Uh-huh.' Blake wondered what kind of parallel universe he was moving in now; this was light years from being the community cop in sleepy old Thames.

They carried on doing the rounds of the neighbours, and Blake was surprised how well Rob knew everyone, given he didn't live there. People seemed to be drawn to the older man, being eager to spend a few minutes chatting, and more than one sought his advice on some aspect of their new life. Rob introduced Blake to everyone, making sure they all knew he was a cop – he had borrowed some clothes from Mark to replace his battered and bloodied uniform, so it wasn't obvious – and that he'd been wounded in battle with a gang of bikers.

The reaction was the same from everyone he met; concern, respect and admiration. Not a single person in the community gave him cause for concern, not a single person seemed edgy about having a cop down the road. Blake felt himself relax and enjoy the opportunity to meet some friendly faces and share a few minutes. He noticed that every house seemed to have a firearm either close by the front door or openly carried, which wasn't surprising given the way things were. It was a hell of a societal change in less than a week though.

Rob took the time to share a smile and a joke with everyone, before moving on to the next house. Blake recognised what he was doing and admired his skill. The networking was a natural fit for Rob, and Blake realised that this was Rob's place in the new world.

While Mark was the muscle, the go-to guy, Rob was the organiser. He was the one that built the relationships they would rely on going forward. The time he spent now should pay dividends in future when things got tougher – and Blake had no doubt that they would indeed get tougher.

They walked back towards home, Blake's arm aching but the fresh air doing him the world of good. The front-slung M4 felt like a natural extension now, after several days of having it practically glued to him.

As they passed the last driveway before the Dobson's, Blake checked out the house. A man and woman were out the front, watching them pass by. He noticed that neither of them was armed. He lifted his hand and waved, but got nothing in return.

'Don't waste your energy,' Rob said, ignoring the couple.

'We're not popping in there?'

Rob gave a dismissive snort. 'When hell freezes over, maybe. Until then, they've got nothing we need and they're not buying what we're selling.'

Blake smiled to himself. His initial evaluation of the man hadn't been wrong; he was a tough old rooster.

39

'You know whatchu gotta do,' Little Dog said.

His breath was hot in Jake's face. Jake could feel the blood pounding in his temples. Needed a smoke to bring his shit down, but no time for that. LD was right; he needed to get this sorted. No room for snitches, no matter who they were. A little part of him, deep down inside, secretly hoped there was an innocent explanation for his Nan's actions. It twisted his gut to think she'd turned on him, but he knew it had to be true.

And as the enforcer, the responsibility fell on him to sort it out.

'All good, Dog,' he rasped.

He turned and ran an eye over the dozen or so men standing nearby. They were all waiting expectantly. All of them were capable of what needed to be done. His eye fell on one, a big boy named Adam. Recently patched and eager to prove himself.

Jake turned back to Little Dog. 'I'll take Ads,' he said.

Little Dog nodded, as if he was agreeing to having a beer.

'Do it,' he said.

Jake caught Ads' eye. 'You're up,' he said, and Ads came forward from the group. He didn't smile, just waited for instructions.

Jake bumped fists with him. 'Got shit to do,' he said.

THE HEAVY FOOTFALLS were the first sign of trouble.

Aroha stirred on the couch, where she'd drifted off some hours ago. She cracked her eyes open to see a large man standing over her. She awoke with a start, not comprehending how or why this man was in her house, but knowing it was trouble.

He put a hand on her bony shoulder and easily held her down on the couch. Aroha recognised him as one of the Bandits, but didn't know his name. He was a big ugly bruiser with a lot of tattoos and a beard.

'Don't be stupid,' the man told her, 'and keep your mouth shut. Unnerstand?'

Aroha nodded, her heart racing. She really needed to pee.

'Where'd you go last night?' the man said. He towered over her, and just his presence was enough to scare her.

Aroha tried to think fast, but she was so scared her brain froze up and she just stared at the man. He repeated the question.

'I...I...no place...'

'Don't lie to me old lady,' the man said. His voice was calm but full of menace. 'We know what you done.'

Aroha's mind went from zero to a million miles an hour as she struggled to catch up with the situation she found herself in. *How could they know where she went? Did someone follow her?*

'I...I dunno what you mean,' she managed.

The man frowned and shook his head.

'I said don't lie,' he growled. 'I'll give you one more chance, but only 'cause you're a old lady.'

Aroha saw movement behind him then Jake appeared behind the man. Her heart leaped for a split-second, thinking he'd come to rescue her from this big brute. All hopes were dashed when she saw him lean casually against the wall and fold his arms, staring at her. He wasn't here to rescue her at all – he was running the show.

'Look at me,' the man said, and Aroha couldn't help but look up. 'Tell me what you did last night. We know you took a horse and were gone all night.' He leaned down so his face was close to hers. 'Did you go and warn that guy we were coming?'

The urge to pee was so strong that Aroha felt herself let go a bit. Her cheeks reddened with the humiliation of wetting herself in front of this man, but in a strange way it hardened her resolve. Aroha had spent many years around men like this, violent men who used their fists before their hearts and minds, men who beat and intimidated women and anyone else who got in the way.

Aroha looked him in the eye.

'I went for a horse ride,' she said fiercely. 'So what?'

The man scowled now, not used to being spoken back to like that. She saw the skin tighten around his eyes.

'Where did you go?' he growled. 'And watch your fuckin' mouth.'

Aroha took a breath and felt a wave of calmness.

'I rode around the countryside,' she said, 'like I did when I was a girl.'

'You're a liar.'

The man's fist shot out so fast she never saw it coming. The punch to her side forced the wind from her lungs and she gasped as pain exploded through her torso. Her head spun and she thought she was going to pass out. She lay there wheezing with the big man still leaning down over her.

'Try again,' he said. 'Did you go and warn that guy?'

Aroha was taking shallow breaths, unable to fill her lungs. She cut her eyes towards him and dragged her dry tongue across her lips.

'You,' she rasped, 'go to hell.'

The man's wide nostrils flared and he straightened up, bunching his fists. He glanced over towards Jake, who watched silently.

Jake gave him a nod and the man turned back to her.

Aroha locked eyes with Jake and held his gaze when the big man hit her again.

40

R ob turned off the generator and waited until it had completely stopped.

It was an older model inverter, and the distinctive throb of the engine was noticeable. Sound carried further at night, so they only ran the unit during the day. There was no point in advertising the fact that they had a resource that others would want – they had already attracted enough attention in the last few days.

Rob sighed and rubbed a hand over his face. He was feeling his age. Since retiring he'd got used to an easy life – no rush to get up in the morning unless they chose to, an afternoon nap if he felt like it, a comfortable house.

Since making the trek to Gemma and Mark's place they had been sleeping badly, not exercising enough, and worrying too much. He was constantly tired and stressed, resulting in his bad turn.

He felt like he needed a long beach holiday, but that wasn't going to happen any time soon. He hitched up his belt, the Browning High Power holstered on his right hip weighing it down more than the spare magazines on the other side.

As always, the Lee Enfield was not far away, leaning against the wall of the garage. Rob sighed again. Even though he'd been a Navy man in his youth, he'd never served in a combat zone. Too young for Vietnam and long gone before the Gulf, he'd never in his wildest dreams imagined that his first taste of action would be on New Zealand soil.

He thought for a moment about the rev-up he'd given Blake. He didn't regret it; the bloke had needed a word. Couldn't have him dragging himself around like some sorry-arsed old dog when the chips were down.

He double-checked the fuel in the genny and closed the closed the garage door. He paused and looked out across the land, feeling the gentle breeze on his face. It was quiet just now, only the rustle of trees in the wind and the snort of the pig as she fed in her sty.

Rob heard footsteps behind him and turned to see Gemma approaching. She looked troubled – didn't they all right now? – and he knew why. She had filled them in on the journey she and Alex had made and he was amazed at what they had been through. His little girl – he could never say his favourite, not out loud – braving streets torn apart by riots and looters and criminals, gun-wielding thugs that tried to hunt them down.

It was a far cry from school lunches and PTA meetings.

'Hey Dad.'

She came in for a hug and he squeezed her tight, just like he had when she was little. Some things never changed. They held each other for a long moment until she pulled away, wiping her eyes.

'What's up?' Rob held her by the shoulders as she brushed her tears away. 'Worried about Mark?'

'Yeah.' Gemma sniffed and got herself together. 'He should be back.'

Rob checked his watch. It was only lunchtime.

'Not yet,' he said. 'Give him time, he'll be back.' He gave her an encouraging smile. 'Don't worry about him Gem, he'll be fine. He can look after himself.'

She nodded, but he could tell she wasn't satisfied.

'I know,' she said. 'But what if...'

He shook his head firmly. 'Not gunna happen, Gem. You've gotta have faith. He's got this far, and got us *all* this far, right? He'll be fine and he'll be back home before you know it.'

She nodded again, and managed a weak smile. 'Of course,' she said.

Rob nodded too, hoping he'd set her anxiety at ease, but knowing that he probably hadn't.

'But if he's not back on time,' Gemma said, 'we go to Plan B.'

'Plan B is what?' he said.

She looked him in the eye, and he saw the determination there.

'We go and find him.'

41

The storage shed they took me to was beside the community hall, and the thug escorting me unlocked the padlock with a key. Once the door was open, I was shoved hard from behind and staggered inside. I tripped over something in the half light and crashed into the wall.

The door closed behind me and I heard the lock click into place.

I looked around and got my bearings. Just a small tin shed, maybe half the size of a single garage. Rough plank shelves, cobwebs and dust everywhere, a few bags of what looked like fertiliser in the corner.

Dirt floor and one grimy window.

I looked around, letting my eyes adjust to the dim interior. There was a long dark shape on the floor and it took me a few moments to realise that I'd tripped over a body. A man in jeans and a black leather vest over a T-shirt, woolly hair, and obvious facial injuries.

I crouched over him and touched the back of my hand to his bare arm. Cold, dead as a doornail.

I peered closer, examining the injuries. Either he'd been hit by a wrecking ball or he'd been beaten to death. Given the surroundings, more likely the second option. As my eyes got more accustomed to the light, I looked closer at his face. Even with the battering he'd taken, I recognised him.

Tintz.

The thug who had been instrumental in my leaving the Police now lay dead at my feet. I stared at him, my mind working hard to fit the pieces into place. I didn't give a shit that he was dead – the world was a better place for it.

But how we came to be in the same place…was I being stitched up somehow? Some people don't believe in coincidences, but I knew that sometimes shit just happened. Fate, nothing to get freaked out about.

I stood up and back, staring at the body. He was a gangster from Papakura, an associate of whichever gang would currently have him. Such a loser that not even a gang would take him on. It wouldn't surprise me if he was now – or had been – knocking around with the Bandits. They were one of the biggest and baddest, and he would be drawn to that. Whether it was them that had killed him was another question.

Ultimately, I decided, who cared? It didn't matter to me that he was dead. All that mattered was how the hell I was going to get out of there.

They had taken all my weapons and gear, giving me a decent pat-down before throwing me in the shed.

One thing they had missed, however, was my pocket knife. I had always carried a small Victorinox Swiss Army knife, just a basic one with a blade, a flat-head screwdriver/bottle opener and a corkscrew. It was an everyday carry item that I used all the time, and I had tucked it into my sock as a back-up.

I took it out now and moved to the window. It was so dirty I could barely see through it, but I could make out a section of long grass then a house, the side of the hall to my left and maybe a fence to the right.

I couldn't see any people, but I could smell cigarette smoke. The window itself was fixed into the frame, so I would have to either break the pane or work it loose somehow to create an opening. Either way would probably attract attention.

The door was tin, like the walls, a standard size and secured from the outside. There was a gap of a couple of inches at the bottom and draughty gaps at the sides. The hinges were on the inside, so potentially I could work those loose and remove the door. Again, it would attract attention.

I prodded the wooden framing with my knife blade, hoping it would be rotten enough to dig the hinge screws out, but it was solid. I would need a chisel. Moving around each wall, I checked the framing, hoping for a rotten piece where I could work some magic and make a hole to escape through, but there was nothing.

If I had a night or two I could probably tunnel under with my tiny knife, but I had no idea how long I would be there for. It was looking more and more likely that the door was the only way out, and I would need someone to open it for me.

Things weren't looking great.

42

B ack when he'd joined the Police, John Blake had never thought he'd last. He'd come in as a fresh-faced nineteen-year-old who had a vague idea of wanting to serve his community in some way, and no real clue as to how.

The military was way too structured and disciplined for him, being the product of an artist and a holistic massage therapist – free-spirited parents who wanted their only child to experience all the beautiful things in the world without shackles. To say they were surprised at their son's career choice was the understatement of the year.

But Blake had further surprised them, and himself, by not only enjoying it but being good at it. He wasn't a hard-arse street cop who chased the adrenaline – Blake liked solving problems and keeping the peace. He found his calling as a community cop, where he could use his people skills to their best advantage.

He bounced around a couple of stations before finding himself in Thames, a small town that served as the centre of the Coromandel, and was ideal for someone like him. He could get out for regular fishing, occasional hunting and the slow pace of life that he enjoyed.

Now, sitting here on the deck at his hosts' house with a cup of coffee, he wondered how the hell things had gone to rat shit so quickly. His arm throbbed but was well-dressed, and his body ached. His mind was racing too, processing everything that had happened.

Never in a million years would he have foreseen the events of the last few days. Going from never even being threatened with a weapon in his life, to shooting it out with a bunch of gangsters on a main highway and seeing his mate die beside him.

Poor Luke; he'd been a good man. A keen musician and great with the kids he worked with.

Blake knew he was lucky not to have fallen beside him – if it hadn't been for the intervention of Mark and Alex, he was sure he would've done. The loss of Luke was like a weight in his chest, crushing down his lungs and making it hard to breathe when he thought about it. He'd woken during the night, breaking a dream that he could no longer recall but that left him feeling panicked and confused.

He never mentioned this to his hosts – he didn't know them, didn't know if they could assist him to deal with the trauma he knew he was suffering.

Blake stroked his hand along the dog's back, Jethro nuzzling against his leg and wagging his tail.

'I think he likes you,' a voice said behind him.

Blake turned in the chair to see Archie coming onto the deck. He had a Spiderman water bottle in one hand and a stick in the other. Blake smiled.

'I reckon he'd like anyone who'll give him a pat,' he said.

'He does like pats,' Archie nodded seriously. 'And sticks.'

He plopped into one of the other chairs at the outdoor table. It was a wooden set with eight chairs and a hole in the table centre for a sun umbrella. The umbrella was packed away until summer rolled around again. Archie took a long draw on his bottle sipper. He looked at Blake.

'Did it hurt?' he said. 'You know, when you got shot?'

Blake paused, surprised by the question and unsure how to answer.

'Yeah,' he said. 'Not so much at first but a lot after, once the adrenaline wore off.'

Archie nodded, taking another sip.

'I heard that it hurts,' he said.

Blake felt himself smile again. Such a serious comment from such a young child. The boy's next comment surprised him more.

'I'm sorry about your friend,' Archie said. 'Dad said he died. He got killed by some bad guys, you know.'

Blake nodded, again unsure how to respond. He hadn't stopped thinking about that event since it happened. As supportive as the Dobson family had been, the sincerity of the little boy's words touched him more than anything else. His throat was tight and he felt his cheeks getting hot.

'Thanks,' he rasped.

'That's okay.' Archie swung his legs, not tall enough to touch the deck from the chair. 'I'm here to help.'

Blake nodded and looked away, his chest fluttering as he battled with his emotions. The light breeze coming across the green paddocks brought the scent of wildflowers and animals and a hint of rain. The sky was overcast, and it was cool enough outside to require a jacket. Blake's fingers settled on the dog's head and scratched behind his ear. He felt his surge of emotion easing and he forced himself to take a breath. Rob's words were still fresh in his mind, and he knew the man was right. He couldn't afford to sit around feeling sorry for himself.

He needed to heal mentally and physically, and he needed to do it fast.

Maybe, right now, sitting here with a young boy and a dog and looking out at a paddock was just what he needed.

43

I hadn't been in the shed for long when I heard footsteps approaching. I tucked the pocket knife back into my sock and stepped away from the door where I'd been listening.

I knew there were at least a couple of guys out there, plus however many had just arrived. No point trying to jump that many; I'd be dead in seconds. I needed an opportunity to get one on his own.

The door swung open and one of the monstrous 'roid-ragers filled the doorway. He shifted his shoulders sideways to get through into the shed. He had a holstered sidearm but his hands were free, and I could guess why.

'How many people at your place?' he said.

I shrugged and shook my head. 'Don't know mate.'

He eyed me, his face blank. 'You got machine guns and shit there?'

I shrugged again. 'Don't know mate.'

'That's two,' he said.

I said nothing.

There was no point arguing with him, and I sure as hell wasn't going to tell him the truth. There was no fucking way I wanted these animals going to my home. It was a catch-22; if I told them the truth, it would sound attractive to them, but if I didn't, they would probably just go anyway. These guys didn't strike me as master tacticians. They had a sniff of something they liked and nothing I said would stop them.

'Last chance bro,' he said. 'You don't gimme answers now, you gonna get hurt.'

I shrugged as if I didn't care, even though I knew he could – and would – seriously hurt me. I sucked down deep breaths, oxygenating my blood. Already the fight-or-flight instinct was kicking in and adrenaline was hitting my bloodstream. Fight-or-flight is fine when you have an option. Unfortunately, I didn't.

The big man took another step into the shed. He rolled his neck and shoulders, popping joints like a string of firecrackers.

'We're goin' to your place,' he said. 'Who we gonna meet there?'

'The Easter bunny,' I said. 'Maybe Santa Claus.'

He almost smiled, then moved so fast I barely even registered it before he hit me. A shoulder charge knocked me back against the wall then he was into me. All I could do was cover up and drop my elbows to try and protect my head and torso as best I could. My best wasn't good enough and he landed punches so fast and hard that I was winded and slipping down the wall in seconds.

Before I even hit the ground the kicks were coming in, mainly to my torso but a couple of decent ones to the head too. My head spun and a guttural growl sounded in my throat. He was either wearing boots or concrete blocks, it was hard to tell, but whatever it was they were doing the business.

I felt my equilibrium rush away from me and knew I would go under if it did. I grabbed it back at the last second and hung on for dear life, even though I had the Fourth of July show performing in front of my eyes and an AC/DC concert going full noise in my head.

I brought my knees up and curled into a ball, kicks and stomps landing in a never-ending blur of brutality. I had no chance to even catch my breath – I just had to hang on and ride it out.

After a lifetime, the big man stopped and stepped back, breathing hard. My own breath was coming in agonising gasps as I struggled to get my lungs working. When I wasn't gasping, I was groaning. Hopefully he got the message that I was fucked and he would lay off.

No such luck.

'Ten minutes, bro,' he said. 'Then we'll try again.'

I heard him move then the door closed. I lay where I was for a few long minutes, trying to get my shit together. It was no easy task when you felt like you'd been hit by a truck then reversed over.

It didn't feel like anything was broken, but that didn't mean I was good to go. My body throbbed all over. I spat a string of thick saliva and forced myself to my knees.

Time was running out fast.

44

Jenny Dobson had never planned on living with Mark and Gemma, not even in poor health or retirement.

He'd always been the more easy-going of her two sons, at least until he reached adulthood. Matthew had been the handful when they were younger, the older brother that had an answer for everything and always pushed the boundaries. Mark had just cruised along, although he'd always had a hell of a stubborn streak in him.

When they reached adulthood, the boys seemed to have swapped roles. Matt settled into the corporate world with a side interest in politics, and Mark went into the Police. Both were ideally suited to their roles, but she had found herself drifting from Mark, particularly after he met Gemma. She was someone that Jenny had been unable to manipulate and she didn't like that. Mark had become more aggressive and strong-minded, and less inclined to compromise or tolerate his mother's attempts at getting her own way.

Needless to say, her stay with them during her kitchen renovations had not been a bundle of laughs. Archie was always entertaining but she wished she had a stronger relationship with him. Unlike Matt's kids, who she had looked after practically every school holidays, she had never even babysat Archie. The little time they'd spent together lately had gone some way to building the relationship, but Jenny knew there was plenty of road ahead. And he was the easier of the three.

Walking down the driveway, she reflected for a moment on the shooting incident at the house. She'd never dreamed she would have to pull a gun to defend her grandson's life, but she'd done it without hesitation. And she knew she would do it again. The only sleep she had lost over the incident had been from worry over it happening again, and time spent assessing herself. She didn't see herself as a killer, and it had nothing to do with being unsure she'd actually killed either of the two young men she'd shot.

She was proud that she had reacted so well and had saved Archie's life, and she knew that the rest of the family – even the McMasters – were proud of her too. It made her feel good; it made her feel *relevant*.

Jenny got to the road and looked right, seeing the roadblock down at the end with a pair of men. She wasn't sure who was on guard duty and couldn't see their guns, but she knew they were there. Another of Mark's ideas. If she didn't know better, she'd say he was paranoid. Mind you, she had to admit that his precautions had paid off so far.

She could see Sophie out in her vegetable garden, bending and picking as Rusty watched over her. He saw her and gave a friendly wave and Jenny waved back.

She felt a lift inside. They were nice people, the Van Dijks. People of her own age that she could happily share a cup of tea with. She was about to cross the road when she saw a flicker of movement in the paddock behind the Van Dijks' house.

Jenny paused, not sure if her eyes were playing tricks or not. She saw it again. Someone moving in the paddock, towards the house, keeping low.

She frowned. There was only the two of them living there, unless they'd had family turn up and she hadn't heard. That seemed unlikely – Jenny liked to keep her finger on the pulse. Besides, if it was a family member, they wouldn't need to move furtively.

She started across the road, the person in the paddock moving out of sight behind the house. She didn't want to yell out and make a scene just in case, so she hurried across the road. Rusty saw her coming and said something. Sophie stood up and turned, smiling. She had a handful of baby potatoes and dropped them in the bowl Rusty was holding.

'Hello Jenny,' Sophie said. 'Look at thesh beautiful potatoesh.'

Jenny crossed the front lawn towards them. 'There's someone sneaking round out the back,' she said hurriedly. 'I saw someone in the paddock.'

They both looked alarmed and Rusty immediately handed the bowl of potatoes to his wife. He started heading towards the rear of the house, and Jenny looked that way, seeing his rifle leaning against the fence a few metres away.

She went after him, Sophie close behind. Rusty went out of sight behind the house and they immediately heard a shout.

'Hey! What're you...'

He was cut off and Jenny heard a crash, a thump and a curse. She reached the back of the house, the property opening out to her right with a patio area and full, well-maintained flower gardens.

Rusty was on the patio, struggling with a woman, their arms locked together as each tried to gain some advantage. A preserving jar lay smashed at their feet, fruit spilled everywhere. Another female was coming out the back door with a bag over her shoulder and a kitchen knife in her hand. Both looked scruffy and Jenny didn't recognise either of them.

'Fuck off, old man,' the second one screeched, coming at Rusty with the knife, 'I'll cut you up!'

Rusty turned to see the new threat and the woman he was struggling with got a hand free. She punched him in the side of the head and Rusty staggered. She kicked him then, landing a good boot to the leg which buckled his knee and sent him to the ground. The second woman came at him, knife raised, and Jenny heard herself shout.

'Hey! Stop that!'

The woman looked her way with a smirk, breaking her stride.

'Yeah, bitch? I'll fuckin' cut you up too.'

Jenny felt her mouth go suddenly dry and stopped where she was. She knew she'd have no chance against a younger woman with a knife. The first one kicked Rusty again and he let out a yell of pain.

'You bloody get out,' came Sophie's voice from behind Jenny. 'Filthy thievesh!'

Sophie came forward beside Jenny, her husband's rifle levelled at the two women.

One of them swore and they both turned and ran, across the back lawn to the rear fence. They were over it and gone into the paddock in seconds.

Rusty picked himself up slowly, rubbing gingerly at his leg. The women helped him to one of the outside chairs and he sat, letting out a groan.

Jenny took the gun from Sophie and put it aside while Sophie tended to her husband. Her heart was racing and a cold sweat had broken out on her brow. Jenny took a moment to gather herself, realising how serious the incident really could have been. By the looks of him, Rusty was going to be sore, but he was lucky not to have a knife buried in his gut.

Jenny leaned against the table and gathered herself. Maybe now they could have that cup of tea.

'WHO ARE THESE PEOPLE?' Alex asked, pacing the Van Dijk's lounge with his hands clasped.

Jenny had just finished her story, and Gemma and Sophie were tending to Rusty. He was at the dining room table with his shirt off, a decent black bruise already showing on his ribs. Nothing was broken but he would be stiff and sore for a good few days.

'Lucky it wasn't worse,' Gemma said, wiping her hands on a tea towel. She gave the older man a smile. 'I think you'll be okay, Rusty.'

'Thank you, Gemma.' He nodded and carefully put his shirt back on with Sophie's help. 'I feel very lucky. I thought that girl...' His voice trailed off and he shook his head. 'I thought she wash going to shtab me.'

Gemma patted his shoulder gently and turned to Sophie and Jenny.

'Bet they hadn't counted on you two being there,' she said.

Sophie didn't smile and Gemma could see she was shaken up by the experience. Jenny put a hand on the other woman's back and said, 'It wasn't me, it was Sophie. They would've had me if they'd had the chance.'

Gemma wasn't so sure, but said nothing. After her mother-in-law's intervention to save Archie, her actions in today's incident weren't really surprising, and she was happy to give credit where it was due.

'So who are these people?' Alex repeated. 'Is it the same people that Mark ran off, the beggars that came around?'

'I don't know,' Gemma said. 'He said it was a woman and a kid, a young girl. This sounds like a couple of teenagers.'

'Could be the same family,' he said, 'or the same group. Might be more than one family.'

'Were they white or Maori?' Gemma asked.

'White girls,' Jenny said. 'Like westies.'

'Probably not from Meremere then,' Gemma said. She wasn't aware of any bogun families in the area, but that meant nothing. 'I hope they're not part of that family that stalked us,' she said to Alex.

He nodded. 'There was a couple of others at the start, wasn't there? The ones with the dog?'

'Yeah, the fat chick and the guy with her. I never saw them after that. Maybe they followed on behind the others?'

Rusty spoke up from the table, where he'd been washing down painkillers and listening.

'I think I may know,' he said. He took a last swallow and put his glass down. 'I heard shome mushic the other night, quite late, coming from over on the nexsht road. I don't know which houshe it wash, but it wash definitely over there. Over the back of here, I'm not sure how far but not too far.'

Gemma nodded. 'And that's something new?' she said. 'You haven't heard it before?'

'Never. Normally it ish very quiet, ash you know.'

Alex caught her eye. 'What are we going to do then?' he said. 'Do we go around there?'

Jenny raised her eyebrows. 'And do what?'

'Well if Mark was here, he would probably just rock around and tell them to pull their heads in,' Gemma said. 'I'm not sure we should do that, though.'

'Wait 'til he gets back?' Jenny suggested. 'I wouldn't want you guys going around there, they're not very nice characters.'

'I agree,' Sophie said. 'I don't think you should go, Gemma.'

'Neither do I,' Gemma said. 'We'll wait for Mark to get back, and see what he says. But we'll let the other neighbours know, and keep an eye out in case they come back. Hopefully they got the message though.'

'I'm sure they did,' Rusty said, smiling at his wife. 'After sheeing thish lady with a rifle, they won't be back.'

As she led the way to the door, Gemma wasn't convinced.

45

It was easy to lose track of time when your day was filled in with getting filled in.

Pua had been back twice since the first beating, and it was rapidly becoming Groundhog Day. He asked me the same questions, gave me the same time frame, and dealt out a beating before leaving again. It felt like forever, but I figured that less than an hour had passed since he first began.

There was just enough time to get my breath back and start to compose myself before he returned.

The door opened and the light was blocked out by a huge frame. I was against the far wall, favouring my tender ribs and taking deep breaths. It always paid to oxygenate your blood before a fight, or in my case, a beating. I let my breath out and looked up, expecting to see Pua giving me that blank, focussed stare that he had.

Dion stared back at me instead, as big as the other man and equally mean-looking. I had pegged them as brothers, and had heard him referred to by name.

'Hello, Dion,' I said.

He stared at me, giving nothing away. It appeared that my

attempts at building a personal connection were not going to work well with him.

'Is it lunchtime yet?' I asked.

He gave a snort and stepped aside. One of the young fellas stepped in, this one holding something in his hand that I couldn't quite see.

'You don't wanna talk?' Dion said.

I managed a shrug. 'I'm happy to talk,' I said. 'I can't tell you what you want me to say, though.'

'Bad luck then,' he said. 'Gonna have to cut you up. Lose a finger or a ear, you might wanna talk.'

He had the same uneducated, rough way of talking as his brother. There was a click and a blade appeared in the young guy's hand.

'Cyrus here got shot up by your friends,' Dion said. The young guy glowered at me. 'They killed his mate. He's not too happy about it, eh.'

I gave a scoff. 'Did he tell you he got shot by a grandma with a shotgun?'

Dion didn't flinch, but I saw a twitch from Cyrus.

'Yeah,' I said, 'she said they were a couple of pussies who pissed themselves and ran away crying.'

Cyrus gave a growl and charged forward, lurching awkwardly as he moved. He swiped at me with the knife and I ducked and weaved, feeling a jolt of pain through my chest from my ribs. I pushed him aside and he hit the wall, but he came back again, swinging wildly with the knife. I slapped his arm away and moved behind him.

Dion stayed at the door, blocking my escape.

Cyrus came at me again, swinging at chest height, and I stumbled as I backed away. I felt myself going down, hit the wall with my shoulder, and Cyrus came at me. I landed on my elbow, he came in with a jab at my gut, and I felt an impact across my ribs as he connected. There was no immediate pain, and I focussed on getting away. He wobbled on his injured leg and I lashed out, hooking his good leg with my foot and sweeping it from under him.

He went down backwards and I scrambled for him, blocking his next slash with my forearm against his. I grabbed his knife hand and twisted hard, wrenching at the weapon. He scrabbled at my hand with his fingers, trying to prise my hand off the knife. I landed a decent punch to his jaw, distracting him long enough to pry the switchblade from his grasp, and he started throwing punches at me. I was on my knees over him, with him on his back, and he couldn't get enough power in his punches to do any damage.

I got a good grip on the knife and slashed it across his forearm, the closest thing I could see. He shrieked and bucked wildly as blood appeared.

A huge boot hit me in the back and knocked me forward as Dion helped him out. The wind exploded from my lungs and I collapsed on top of the young guy, across his legs, gasping for breath.

I was only partially conscious of the knife sinking in beneath me but I heard Cyrus' reaction, a wild scream that deafened my left ear. He bucked me off and I rolled to the side, the knife going with me. When I rolled away, the blade came free from his thigh and unblocked the deep hole it had made.

Arterial blood jetted across the shed and hit the far wall, powerful spurts bursting forth as his panicked heart worked hard to circulate the blood around his body. Unfortunately for him, by freakish luck, I had jabbed his own blade straight into his femoral artery.

I lay on my side and gasped for air, while Cyrus screamed the house down and watched his life force decorate the wall and ceiling. Dion stood with his mouth open, not knowing what the hell to do, and I became aware of others crowding into the shed. No one gave me a second look, just left me to sort myself out while they tried to stem the blood flow from Cyrus' leg.

Even in the state I was in, I knew there was no point. He needed urgent medical attention and someone to hold the fort until that arrived, but he had neither option.

One of the Bandits was yelling at him to shut up, while someone else was trying to apply pressure to his wound.

I saw him shuddering and trying to speak, and knew he was gone.

I got enough breath in my lungs to get onto my knees, and I stayed there, watching. I was in no shape to help them, even if I'd wanted to.

It was all over in seconds. Before I'd even drawn my first full breath, Cyrus lay still on the dirt floor, his sightless eyes staring at the wall. One of the Bandits had blood all over his arms and the front of his gang T-shirt, and looked like he was going into shock.

I ignored them and concentrated on getting myself together. My back throbbed all over from the kick and I was pretty sure there was at least a sprain there somewhere. I checked my ribs and found a shallow slice, just enough to open up the skin and make it bleed a lot, but fortunately not a puncture wound. Even so, it would need some attention soon, and some butterfly strips or stitches to close it up.

'The fuck went wrong here?' Jake demanded as he shouldered his way through his thugs. He stared down at Cyrus' body then at me, and back to Dion.

Dion showed no emotion at all. 'He got the upper hand, Jake. Lucky shot in the leg, got an artery.'

Jake scowled hard and fixed on me. 'Motherfucker,' he growled. 'You're causin' us problems we don't need.'

I kept my mouth shut, mentally preparing myself for the beating that was sure to follow. There was no point provoking him now with a smart-arse comment.

'Tie him up,' Jake ordered. 'He ain't goin' nowhere.' He turned to Dion. 'Come on, we got shit to do.'

46

'It's getting out of control, Dad.' There was a waver in Gemma's voice, but her face was stoic.

He frowned as he listened. He didn't like it that Rusty and Sophie had been subjected to an attack either, and his gut reaction was that someone needed their arse kicked. But he was also realistic enough to know he wasn't the guy to do it.

'We need Mark home.'

Rob nodded his agreement. It was also time; he should've been home by now. The fact that he was still out there was another worry, piled on top of the rest. The pile was getting higher every day.

'We can't have people thinking we're a soft touch,' he agreed. 'And Rusty and Sophie are vulnerable over there, even with us across the road.'

'We don't want to be going to war,' Sandy interjected. Neither of them had seen her appear in the lounge doorway, but she'd heard enough of their conversation to know where it was going.

Rob turned to look at her.

'We're not going to war, my girl,' he said. 'We're just concerned about the neighbours, and what's going on around here.' He glanced at his daughter then back to his wife. 'And concerned about our own family.'

Sandy looked past him to Gemma, who stood with her arms folded and her jaw set. She hadn't been close to her father as a teenager, but Sandy knew they were similar in so many ways. Not least their bloody-mindedness.

'So what're you going to do?' Sandy said, her throat tight and dry.

'I'm going to find Mark,' Gemma said firmly. 'Then we're going to have to do something about those mongrels over the way.'

47

It was thirty years since Aroha had been beaten like that. The last time was from a partner who had a drinking problem, anger issues, a gambling addiction and short man's disease.

The relationship had lasted twelve years, and he'd let fly with his fists at least once a week from about a month into it. She'd stayed with him, beaten down emotionally and psychologically broken, until the bastard had died.

He and his buddies had burgled a warehouse but got sprung by a security guard. The truck had taken off and he'd forgotten to hang on, fell off the back and cracked his skull.

Aroha got the news from a sombre-looking cop a few hours later, and had struggled to keep the smile from her face. She'd downed a bottle of beer, smoked a joint and thanked her lucky stars. She'd never looked back, and swore she'd never be treated like that again.

Now, shuffling across the kitchen floor one painful inch at a time, she held her ribs gingerly and took shallow breaths. By God, it hurt. She'd wet herself and felt ashamed, but she was still alive.

Jake hadn't even come and checked on her before he and the big thug had left her house. After all she'd done for him all these years, not even checking she was still breathing. Maybe that was the point; maybe she was supposed to be dead. Maybe he didn't care either way.

She got to the bench and leaned heavily against it, wheezing. Just moving this far from the couch had made her head spin and she felt like she was going to pass out. She got her fingers round the glass of water she'd left there earlier, and raised it shakily to her lips. Some slopped down her chin but she managed to get a drink, took a breath, and emptied the glass.

Holding there for a few minutes, Aroha made two decisions. Firstly, she couldn't trust anyone here. Secondly, she needed to get the hell out of here.

As battered and broken as she felt right now, that seemed as likely as unicorns and fairies.

48

The holstered Browning went on Gemma's right hip and the spare magazines for it on the left hip.

Beside the mag pouch was another pouch, originally GI-issue for M16 magazines. Now it was stuffed with loose rounds plus a box of .357 Magnum. Gemma figured that if she went through all the ammo in that pouch then she was in serious trouble and would just have to revert to the pistol her Dad had loaned her.

'Have you got enough ammunition, young fella?' Rob was asking Alex, who was gearing up beside her in the garage.

'About as much as I can carry,' Alex said, checking his pockets and the bum bag he wore. The magazines for his Marlin carbine were all loaded and he had a couple of spare boxes – another hundred rounds – in case he needed to refill.

Gemma noticed her Dad frown but say nothing, probably thinking the younger man could always carry more. She wasn't too concerned herself; between them they had plenty of ammo and, all going well, they would probably run into Mark coming back anyway and it would be a wasted trip.

'Got your bags sorted?' Rob said, nudging the day packs on the floor with his boot.

'Yes, Dad.' Gemma adjusted her belt and picked up her day pack.

Each of them was taking some snacks and water, a first aid kit, a rain jacket and a few other bits and pieces that might come in handy. Gemma had packed as if they were going for a short bush walk, even though they were taking the truck. She knew from experience that it paid to be prepared.

'Don't "Yes, Dad" me, missy,' Rob grumbled. 'Just make sure you've got everything you need. Keep yourselves safe.'

She almost said "Yes, Dad" again, but caught herself in time. She knew this mood – her Dad had been the same when she and Mark had gone on their OE. So young and carefree back then. And here he was, still worrying about her.

'It'll be okay,' she said, giving him a hug. 'We'll be back before you know it.'

'Why don't you take one of the other guns?' Rob said. 'Something with more punch than that cowboy gun?'

'I know how to use it,' Gemma said. 'I don't know how to shoot one of those other ones, and I haven't got time to learn now.' He opened his mouth to argue and she cut him off. 'Dad, I don't have time. I promise I'll learn later, okay? But right now, we need to get going.'

He relented and walked them out to the Navara.

'And what's our back-up plan?' Rob said, taking her day pack from her and putting it in the back seat. 'How long do we give you until we come looking?'

Gemma turned to him. 'You don't, Dad,' she said softly. 'We can't keep chasing after each other; nobody will be left at home.'

'I can't just leave you,' he insisted, and she could hear the fear in his voice.

'Dad,' Gemma said firmly, looking him in the eye. 'We need to go and see if we can find Mark. If we can't, well...I don't know. We come back and wait here for him to turn up. We're not going to be long.'

'How long?'

She shook her head. 'I don't know. Probably a couple of hours or so; I don't know.' She could see he wanted to argue but she cut him off with a kiss on the cheek. 'We'll be back soon.'

Rob grabbed her to him, hugging her tightly. 'You better be,' he rasped.

Archie came running over with Jethro in tow and pushed in to give her a big hug, then gave Alex a high five.

'Are you going to pick Dad up now?' he asked, running his eye over their weapons and gear.

'Yep.' Gemma smiled and gave him a big kiss on the cheek. 'See you soon. Look after all your grandparents, and John.'

'I will.' He stood with Rob and waved as the truck headed down the driveway.

Gemma watched him in the rear view mirror, feeling a lump in her throat. She hoped it wouldn't be the last time she saw either of them.

They made their way quickly through Mercer, both noticing how quiet it was. No one out and about, no twitching curtains, not even a dog out on the road.

'It's like a ghost town,' Alex said, keeping a careful eye out while Gemma drove. 'I wonder if anyone's still here.'

Gemma concentrated on the road, giving it some gas and winding her way up the hill towards the place where Mark had told them he would leave the quad bike. They parked up and found the Honda quad soon enough, just as he'd said it would be. Gemma felt a pang of fear. If he hadn't made it back to the bike yet, then he was still on foot somewhere. It spelled trouble and she couldn't help but wonder if they would be walking into a trap.

Or finding Mark's body somewhere.

She tried to push the thought aside but it hung there in the back of her mind, a dark shadow over her. She suddenly doubted whether they should be doing this at all. What if things went wrong and Archie was left orphaned? It went directly against the agreement she and Mark had made, that they wouldn't leave Archie like that.

She felt Alex's eyes on her.

'You okay?' he said softly.

She nodded, her face hot. Sweat was breaking out on her back.

'It's going to be okay,' Alex said. 'We'll be careful. Come on, let's go.'

Gemma nodded again and took a deep breath. She had the feeling they were heading for trouble, but she couldn't leave Mark out there on his own. She and Alex were the obvious choices to come away on a rescue mission, and that's all there was to it. And if – when, she guessed – they came up against some opposition, they would just have to fight harder to make sure they got out.

'Let's go,' she said.

49

T wo Panadol and half a bottle of warm beer later, Aroha managed to make it to her garden.

The fresh air gave her a lift, but her attention was immediately caught by the hum of activity outside the community hall. Engines were idling and men were talking; not the men from the village, but the gangsters that Jake hung with. *Bandits.* The mean sons of bitches that had come and raped her little town.

Standing behind her low front fence, Aroha watched them. There seemed to be an awful lot of them now. The hall was full of them from what she could see, and more were outside, lounging around smoking and laughing. Further down the road, at the bottom of the main street, was an empty section and she could see more men hanging out there. Most of them wore prison-issue grey sweats and green T-shirts.

None of them took any notice of her.

Aroha watched the Bandits outside the hall gathering around a central figure at the door, a hush falling over them as they listened. She felt eyes on her and turned to see her neighbour staring at her from his own front yard. He was an older man but younger than her, and had lived next door for close to twenty years.

'Alright, Aroha?' he called out softly, keeping his voice down so the gangsters didn't hear him.

Aroha set her jaw and gave a short nod. 'Kingi.'

She saw the sadness in his face, the shame. Shame at not stepping in to help his neighbour when she needed him. Aroha felt a lump in her throat. How could an old man step in against men like this? How could *anyone*?

Aroha took another shallow breath and met Kingi's eye again.

'I'll survive,' she said quietly.

Kingi ambled over to the fence separating them and leaned against it so they were only a few feet apart.

'They're bloody bad men, girl,' he said quietly. 'Bloody bad men.'

'My Jake's one of them,' Aroha said, the effort of speaking causing her ribs to cry out.

Kingi nodded slowly, his wrinkled eyes sad. 'He come over, eh?'

'Aye.' Aroha felt a sudden wave of sadness at the thought. Jake had done this as much as the big man had done it.

'They got a fulla.' Kingi jerked a thumb across the road. 'Some cop snuck in and they smashed him over.'

Aroha cocked her head, her curiosity pricked. She hoped her suspicion was wrong but her gut told her it wasn't.

'Did they kill him?' she asked, but Kingi shook his head.

'Na, they're takin' him. He beat up some young fullas they reckon. Takin' him to Tuakau, eh.'

It was him, Aroha knew it. He was here and they were going to kill him, she knew that without a doubt.

'Why Tuakau?'

'Dunno.' Kingi shrugged. 'Heard some o' them talking, said the boys are up at the college there. Must be more of them, s'pose.'

Aroha chewed that over for a moment. It made sense. Jake had more family in Pukekohe and Tuakau. Maybe it was them. Either way, she knew it would be Tuakau College they were going to; it was the only high school in the area ever referred to as a college.

The huddle across the road broke up and men started moving off towards the vehicles. Aroha saw the president getting into a white

Range Rover with one of the two massive Island boys. As the men moved off she saw Jake by the door, looking her way. They locked eyes across the way, holding the stare until he slid on his sharkies and stepped away.

Aroha clenched her jaw. So that's how it was going to be. Well she wouldn't take this lying down.

THE SUN WAS high and there was a light breeze as I was manhandled from the shed. My hands were tied with rough baling twine behind my back, tight enough that I could feel my hands tingling from lack of blood.

Pua moved me on his own, gripping my bicep hard and steering me to the road where a pair of gangsters sitting on hogs waited with a jacked-up black Ranger ute and an ice-white Range Rover.

Little Dog buzzed the rear window down on the Rover. He removed his gold-framed aviators and squinted at me, saying nothing for a few moments. Then he licked his lips and sniffed.

'You killed one o' my boys,' he said coolly.

I said nothing. Beyond him I could see Dion behind the wheel. The engine was running, a soft rumble I could barely hear.

'You think that you holding out on us is gonna stop us from doing what we do?' he said. 'Ain't gonna work like that, bro. We know you got guns and supplies and shit we need, see? So we gonna go take it.'

I stayed silent. At this point in time, the only thing I had control over was myself.

'Problem you got is, when my dogs off the leash, I got no control over them, eh? They get to your place, they gonna rip it apart. Anyone get in their way, they gonna get dead. See what I'm sayin', bro?'

It was hard not to. I stayed quiet, and he narrowed his eyes at me.

'Any sluts there, they gonna get fucked up.'

He waited for a reaction, but I stayed in check. No point in giving him something to feed off. I may have seemed clam on the outside, but I was mentally shitting myself. I knew what these guys were like, what they were capable of.

He wasn't lying when he said people would get fucked up; I just had to hope it was them and not us. We had enough capable shooters at home that could put up a decent fight. I only hoped it wouldn't come to that.

Little Dog sniffed again, then wiped his nose on his sleeve.

'You gonna tell us what we wanna know?' he said.

I eyed him and slowly shook my head.

He nodded and looked past me; decision made.

'Sort 'im out, boys,' he said.

The window buzzed back up and the Range Rover began to move off. Pua jerked me by the arm, steering me towards the two Harleys. One of the riders revved his engine, giving that distinctive roar that only a Harley Davidson motorcycle had.

I had a sudden fear of being hooked up behind a bike and dragged down the road, as the Bandits had been known to do to enemies before. I reflexively pulled away but Pua's grip was unbreakable and he easily kept me moving, putting his other hand on the back of my neck for good measure.

We reached the black Ranger and he lowered the tailgate and told me to get up. I awkwardly tried to climb up and he helped me along my way, lifting me by my legs and unceremoniously dumping me in the tray. He shoved me hard and my skull collided with the back of the cab.

The tailgate slammed shut and the engine started and the two bikes roared. I rolled into a sitting position and watched as we did a u-turn and headed south down the main drag. I knew that this way would take us out to the highway and either north towards Auckland or south towards Huntly. I could see two heads in the cab of the Ranger. One of the bikes was ahead of us and the other fell in behind. Trailing behind that came another ute with several dudes in the back, then a car behind that.

Wherever we were going, they were sending plenty of muscle. I figured that probably wasn't a good thing for me.

50

Gemma and Alex had quickly reached the waste ground at the edge of town, not wasting any time as they raced through the undergrowth. She hoped they wouldn't run into an ambush and her fear for her husband drove her on, desperate to find him and get home again.

Pausing in the last line of undergrowth to catch their breath, they scanned ahead for any threats. At this point in time, Gemma believed anybody in Meremere probably posed a threat to them, at the very least because they would raise the alarm.

The waste ground was home to a couple of wrecked cars and a lot of weeds and, just as Mark had done not long prior, Gemma plotted out their next move. They should be able to get across to the fences without being seen, maybe using the closest wreck as cover.

She turned to share her plan with Alex, and found him carefully studying the wreck nearest to them.

'What is it?' she whispered.

'There's someone in that car,' he breathed.

He burrowed in his bag and came up with a compact pair of binoculars he had borrowed. He focussed on the car again and held it there for a long minute. Finally he lowered them and turned to her.

'I think he might have Mark's bag,' he said softly.

Gemma snatched the binos from him and glued them to her eyes, zooming in to get a good look. She could see what looked like a homeless guy lounging in the back seat of the abandoned car, rummaging through a bag. He was pulling out various bits of gear, and she immediately recognised Mark's drink bottle. Her stomach dropped and she felt panic rise in her chest. She focussed on the bag and confirmed it was the day pack her husband had taken earlier that day.

'Oh shit,' she muttered, passing the binoculars back to Alex. 'Oh shit, oh shit, oh shit.'

He waited, watching her. She swallowed hard, forcing the panic down, and took in a deep breath. If this guy had Mark's gear then something had gone horribly wrong. She couldn't see any guns, but maybe somebody else had them. The thought that Mark might be dead was hammering inside her head. Maybe he wasn't, but she knew he wouldn't have given up his gear easily.

Either way, she had to know.

'What d'you want to do?' Alex whispered.

'We still need to find him,' she replied. 'I'm not leaving him.'

Alex put a gentle hand on her arm. 'I hate to say it Gemma...'

'Don't,' she snapped. 'I know, okay? I know. But we still have to check.'

Without waiting for more conversation, she pushed up and set off in a crouched run across the rough waste ground, heading for the car wreck.

Alex followed behind, covering all sides as she focussed on the target ahead.

The guy in the back of the car didn't see her until she was nearly on him, and he jumped with fright as the armed woman appeared seemingly from nowhere.

'Whaddafuck?' he cried, trying to scramble backwards out of the car.

He dropped the day pack as he moved and Gemma grabbed at his leg through the open space where a door once had been. He kicked out at her and she recoiled then lunged forward, ramming the Rossi at him. The barrel caught him in the mouth and he let out an agonised cry, blood coming immediately.

He was too busy with his broken teeth to fight back, and she went around the car, grabbed him by the scruff of his dirty hoody, and jerked him half out of the car. He cried out again, spitting out a tooth, and blood spilled over his chin and neck. He was on his back with his upper torso hanging out of the car, looking at her with fearful eyes.

Gemma pointed the rifle at his face.

'Where did you get that bag?' she hissed.

He garbled something incomprehensible and she touched the muzzle to his forehead.

'Where did you get it?'

'I gave...got...they gave it. They gave it.'

'Who?'

He waved a bloodied finger vaguely away from him.

'Them...y'know...fuck, the dudes...big dudes.'

'Where's the man it came from?'

He looked away and put a hand to his mouth.

'Fuck...broke my teeth, bro...wha' fuck you do that for?'

'Where's he gone?' Gemma put some pressure on the muzzle against his forehead. 'What happened to the man?'

'I dunno...'

'Don't fuckin' lie or I'll blow your fuckin' brains out right here,' she hissed, an anger she had never felt before rising in her. Her finger slipped into the trigger guard. 'Tell me now or you're fuckin' dead.'

His eyes bugged and she smelt a sudden waft of urine.

'They...the big dudes...they took him...in the town.'

Gemma ran her gaze over the interior of the car wreck, spotting bits of tinfoil on the floor, a spray paint can, and several used plastic bags. It smelled of solvents and body odour.

'You live in here?' she said.

The guy shrugged and nodded at the same time.

'Sorta.'

'Was the man hurt?'

The guy shrugged and looked away.

'Maybe, I dunno. A bit.'

'Yes or no?'

He gave a slight nod.

'They give him a bash, eh...bit of a bash.' He felt the rifle muzzle pressing down on his forehead and his eyes bugged again. 'Din't kill 'im though, ain't kill 'im.'

Gemma let her breath out without realising she'd been holding it. He wasn't dead – that was a good start.

'How long ago?' she said. 'How long ago did you see him?'

The guy looked confused, and she realised it was a pointless question. With the solvents and drugs in this guy's system, he wouldn't even know what day it was. That of course affected his reliability, but she had nothing else, so she was prepared to believe what he had said so far.

'Last question,' she said. 'Who are these guys?'

The guy licked his split lip gingerly. He squinted up at her like she was stupid.

'Bandits, bro,' he said. 'They're the Bandits.'

Gemma shifted her gaze to Alex, catching his eye.

'Come and give me a hand.'

The guy didn't resist as they tied his wrists and ankles with para cord, securing him across the back seat. Gemma found a discarded rag in the wreck and tied that around his head, gagging him so he couldn't raise the alarm. All going well, they would release him on their way back.

She turned to Alex, adjusting the day pack on her back.

'Good to go?' she said, and he nodded.

Gemma gave the bound man a last look. He appeared to be nodding off to sleep.

'Let's go,' she said.

51

I estimated we had been on the move for maybe half an hour, most of it spent heading north on the highway. The trip was slowed by having to work a way around the crashed and abandoned vehicles.

I recognised landmarks and saw road signs as we went, and wondered where we were heading to. The further we travelled the longer it would take me to get back, and I was determined to do that. The only way they could stop me would be to kill me, although that seemed a realistic prospect.

There was no way I could escape from the back of the ute as it was moving. Jumping off with my hands tied would be suicide, and if I somehow miraculously made it, there were several vehicles and motorbikes coming behind which would quickly sort me out.

The only thing I could do was wait until we reached our destination, then play the cards I was dealt.

I sat back against the side and got as comfortable as I could, letting my mind drift. Seeing Tintz' dead body had brought back a flood of memories, most of them bad. Disappointment in myself. Anger at him. Resentment of the system. I wondered what had brought about his demise.

He'd always been one of those guys destined for a sad or violent ending. How it came to be that we crossed paths again was a mystery to me, but it didn't really matter. He was dead; I wasn't. Unfortunately, I'd tangled with guys that he either crossed or was a part of, which probably wasn't surprising given the small country we lived in. People talked about there being six degrees of separation between everyone; in New Zealand that was about two degrees.

I'd once arrested a guy who turned out to be the step-brother of an old girlfriend of mine, who turned out to live a street away from us, unbeknown to me. It wasn't an unusual occurrence.

My most pressing issue was how to get out of the situation I was currently in. The Bandits hadn't found the small pocket knife in my boot, but I also couldn't reach it without drawing the attention of my captors. I would need to wait until I was alone to get it, and should then be able to cut my bonds. At least I would then have it available as a weapon. My priority though would be getting away, not fighting. If I could escape without incident, I'd be happy.

The truck took an off-ramp and I fell on my side, missing the sign. It was on a sealed road and I could see the tops of buildings as we whizzed by. We picked up speed again and I managed to get back into a sitting position. I realised we were coming through the small town of Pokeno, and had turned onto the back road leading towards Tuakau, heading north-west.

I didn't know of any Bandits foothold in Tuakau, but that could have changed in the last few days. Or we could be heading past it to Pukekohe, where they certainly had some presence. The convoy of vehicles took the bypass around the town, turned right onto Buckland Road which was the main route to Pukekohe, and headed that way. Tuakau town lay over to the right, and I could see activity at the houses we passed.

The superette at this end of town had been looted and smashed up, and rubbish was strewn about.

Nobody made any attempt to stop the convoy as it raced by, and I was confident we were travelling further on. It came as a surprise when the brakes went on and we turned into the car park of the high school.

I could see other vehicles there now, several hoods standing around smoking. A few openly carried firearms, others had bats or lengths of wood.

I didn't see any gang patches, but they clearly weren't there for a tea party.

As we came to a halt, my gaze fell on two men I recognised, leaning against a primer-grey Ford Falcon. One had his leg in a brace. He saw me and nudged the guy beside him, who turned to look. A smirk came across the second guy's face.

It was the Roimata boys I'd tangled with at the Mitre 10, back on day one of this national emergency. Things had got rough and they'd come off second best. Naturally they were happy to see me now, tied up and held prisoner.

I took a deep breath to calm my nerves. My bad day had just got worse.

52

T he empty section of waste land led to a residential cul-de-sac, and Gemma could see kids playing on the road.

She hunkered down at the corner of the fence and considered their options. She worked out that they couldn't get further into the town without exposing themselves, but to do that would be inviting attack. She wondered if it was at this point that Mark had got captured. There was no point in coming this far and not gathering any intelligence, but neither did she want to walk into trouble.

'This way,' Alex whispered, pointing towards the woods on their left.

He indicated a route through there to circumvent the open ground before them. He looked to her for confirmation, and she nodded. They were just starting to move off when she spotted movement behind them, back where they had broken cover to approach the wrecked car.

'Down.'

She dropped down, bringing the Rossi up in the aim as she saw a person appear at the edge of the undergrowth. Zeroing in through the scope, she recognised the old lady who had come to warn them.

Aroha, in a yellow cardigan and holding herself carefully, as if she was in pain.

The old woman looked around, taking her time, then ran a hand over her face and shook her head. Gemma sensed her frustration, and wondered what she was doing there. It seemed odd for her to pop out of the bush like that.

Gemma raised herself up to a crouch and waved, catching the old woman's eye just as she started to turn away. Aroha stopped and looked hard, then a look of recognition crossed her face and she waved back, gesturing for Gemma to come to her.

Gemma nudged Alex. 'Come on.'

They hurried across to her and moved into the cover of the trees, Aroha following them. Up close, Gemma could now see the old woman was injured. She was holding herself stiffly, and there was clear bruising to her eye.

'What happened?' Gemma asked with a frown.

Aroha shrugged awkwardly.

'They slapped me around,' she said, her voice tight. 'Saw me come back on the horse, wanted to know where I'd gone.' She paused to take a laboured breath. 'They didn't believe me, what I said. So here I am.'

'Where were you going?' Gemma said. 'Did you escape them?'

Aroha's eyes were wet and her bottom lip trembled.

'I was going to come to you,' she said. 'I can't stay here with all this violence going on.' She shook her head. 'This is not my home no more.'

Gemma felt her heart go out to the old woman.

'Have you got the horse here?' she asked, and Aroha shook her head.

'No. I'm walking. I thought your husband would come this way so I went down the track. I found his truck and that quad bike, but no keys.' She gave another awkward shrug. 'I was gonna walk to your place, but I thought I better check 'cause someone must've come with him to have two cars.'

Gemma shook her head in amazement.

'You can come back with us in the truck,' she said. 'We brought it here. Did you see Mark?'

Aroha nodded.

'They took him,' she said. 'I think they're gonna kill him.'

Gemma felt a punch in her chest, even though the news wasn't a surprise.

'Where is he?' she said. 'Where did they take him?'

'Tuakau.' Aroha paused to take a shuddering breath, wincing with pain. 'They gone to meet some others, I don't know who. Might be the *whanau* from Pukekohe though.' Her rheumy brown eyes fixed on Gemma's face. 'They said he beat a couple of the boys up, few days ago. Beat them up quite bad.'

Gemma nodded. She knew about that.

'So they're going to kill him for that?' she said, and Aroha nodded.

'The Roimata boys,' she said. 'They're related to Jake, his nephews.'

'Who's Jake?'

'My grandson.' Aroha's face saddened again. 'He's normally a good boy, but he's back in with those boys again, those Bandits. Bloody *Bandits*.' She spat the word out. 'They're all shits, that's what they are. Things are bad enough without their carry-on, eh?'

Gemma nodded, her mind racing.

'How long ago did they leave?' she asked.

'Ooh, maybe twenty minutes, half an hour. I left as soon as I heard them getting ready to go, and I heard them go.'

'Do you know where they would take him in Tuakau? Is there a house or something there that they'd go to?'

'The school,' Aroha said emphatically. 'I know they done stuff at the college before, meet-ups and suchlike. I think they would go there.'

Gemma nodded, her mind made up.

'We need to move,' she said.

They headed down the track, unaware of the hidden watchers that followed their every move.

53

The president was there, surrounded by adulating sycophants and loving it.

I watched as Jake went and spoke to him. There was a lot of nodding. I scanned around, trying to work out the shortest distance to cover. It didn't look promising. I also checked out the thugs with weapons, trying to suss out who I could disarm the easiest, but that didn't look promising either.

Whatever happened, I would probably need to play it out on the ground and seize whatever opportunity came my way.

Jake broke away and started directing his troops. The ute started up and I was driven through the school to the sports field. We pulled up and the guys in the cab got out, grabbed me from behind and dragged me backwards over the side.

My arms and shoulders took a good scraping on the way and they dumped me on the ground, dropping me as soon as my body cleared the side of the tray. A jolt of pain shot through my shoulder and neck when I hit the deck, and the guys both chuckled at my groans. They gave me a few kicks to the back and guts for good measure, softening me up for what was to come.

Vehicles roared and rumbled all around, a cacophony of noise that overrode all other senses. The ute moved off and I saw the slimmest of opportunities, not being guarded for a moment.

I struggled into a sitting position then rolled to my feet, looking towards the closest classroom, still a good forty metres or so away. I was just starting to move when I was hit with a stiff-arm to the back of my head. It sent me staggering forward then down, tumbling to the ground with no chance of stopping myself.

I lay there while the earth spun, the smell of dirt and petrol fumes in my nostrils, the feel of prickly grass on my cheek. I sucked in a breath, then another, doing whatever I could to get my shit together.

A shadow fell over me and I looked up.

'Get up,' Jake said.

He stood over me, right in my personal space as I got to my feet. We were nose to nose when I straightened up and the booze and cigarettes on his breath washed over my face.

'You wanna get outta here?' he said.

I gave him the slightest nod. His grin exposed stained teeth.

'Ain't gonna happen. Two ways you can die today,' he said. 'Fast or slow.'

I gave nothing away, but my mind churned faster. Neither was a great option.

'And how's that work?' I said.

He grinned again, his dark eyes glittering.

'You wanna go quick, I'll put a bullet in your fuckin' brain right now.'

'And the other option?'

'You think you're a hard-ass? You smashed up my boys, fucked them up pretty bad with a baseball bat.'

I cut my eyes over to the two he was referring to. Both were giving me the evils, as if it was them that I would be fighting. They obviously felt tough surrounded by their mates. This was how these guys rolled – blood sport was their thing. Brutality was a badge of manliness.

Jake spoke again, bringing my attention back to him.

'You go one-out with two of the boys; you win, you get a bullet to the head anyways. You lose...' He shrugged. 'You die slow.'

I raised an eyebrow. 'Since when is two on one a one-out?'

He shrugged again. 'Take it or leave it.' He drew a Sig from his belt and pressed it against the side of my head. 'Or I can just do it now.'

I resisted the urge to pull away from the gun and held his gaze instead. There was no way I was backing down to this piece of shit.

'Untie me then,' I said. 'Let's do it.'

THE NISSAN NAVARA was a powerful truck and Gemma had never had cause to give it a blowout before, but all that changed.

She drove fast and hard from Mercer, mindful of Aroha strapped into the back seat of the double cab, but not letting that slow her down. They flew up the highway, dodging abandoned and crashed vehicles as they chased the convoy of vehicles that Aroha had described. It felt like a race against time, a race to save Mark's life before the gang of thugs dealt to him.

Gemma had never been involved in this sort of incident before, but a lot of things had changed in the last few days. *She* had changed, she knew that without a doubt. Even Alex had changed. Gone was the mild-mannered IT geek, replaced by a guy who had killed and fought his way to freedom as the city burned and fell apart. He was beside her now, his Marlin carbine at the ready, game face on. Heading into a situation against a bunch of gangsters, she would rather have had Mark at her side, but that was the whole point.

She flicked to the speedo for a moment, clocking it at one-fifty. She'd never driven 150 km/h in her life, barely even broke the speed limit.

Today was different, she reasoned. Today it was life or death.

JAKE STEPPED BACK and watched while I was freed.

I looked around at the assembled thugs. There had to be thirty or more of them, at least half of them fully patched, the rest wearing either vests with prospect badges or supporter T-shirts. They were eager for blood and comments and threats were coming my way. Several of them were swigging from bottles and a few pipes were being passed around.

Standing here on the sports field, with motorbikes and cars enclosing us, there was nowhere to run to. I could see armed men on the outside of the circle, one standing up on the back of the ute I had arrived in, obviously keeping guard. Even if I could run, I wouldn't get far.

I watched as Jake consulted Little Dog again, taking the opportunity to roll my shoulders, neck and wrists, loosening up. I shook my legs out. Focussing on getting home gave me a purpose, and to get through this fight, I would need all the mental strength I had.

I'd been in many fights and scraps over the years – it was part of life as a street cop. But I knew this would be different, and I had two challenges to overcome. Firstly, surviving the fight itself. Secondly, escaping with my life afterwards.

I had managed to slip the small pocket knife into my hand and kept it concealed there. If I had the chance to use it, it could be the difference between living and dying.

Jake stepped away from the president, taking position in the middle of the circle so everyone could hear.

'This is a fight to the death,' he announced. 'If the pigshit goes down, he dies. He don't die, there's gotta be two dead Bandits on the floor.' He grinned at the flunkies around him. 'And there ain't gunna be two dead Bandits, eh?'

They roared their approval, giving the usual "Bandits forever, forever Bandits" bullshit. It was an intimidating scene to be the centre of, and I zeroed in, oxygenating my blood with long, slow breaths and visualising the moves I could make.

It would be crucial to get the upper hand early, and that meant someone had to go down fast. With two on one it would over quickly if they got the advantage.

'Zeke,' Jake called, and a long-haired young prospect with a beard and boob tats lurched forward. He was slightly hunched and held his arms out like was carrying basketballs.

'Pua.'

This guy was a different story, and I had guessed he'd be one of the two fighters. He moved efficiently and I could tell he had some fighting experience. Zeke was there to prove himself; Pua was there to finish it.

They came out into the circle and loosened up, Zeke making a show of cracking his knuckles and flexing his hands. Pua eyeballed me and rolled his neck and shoulders, every movement making a solid muscle ripple and roll.

I pointed at the two Roimata boys.

'These two don't want to finish what they tried to start?'

They both glared at me but said nothing. Jake ignored my comment, so I pushed him with another.

'You think these boys will win?' I said.

Jake looked at me like I was raving mad, saying nothing. I repeated my question.

'Course,' he said.

'Then the winner walks free,' I said. I held his gaze. 'You're so confident, should be no issue. Do you back them or not?'

I could see the cogs turning in his head, and he turned towards Little Dog, looking for a lead from his president.

Little Dog nodded without hesitation, and Jake turned back to me.

'It's on,' he said.

I sucked down a long breath and let it out slowly. One hurdle down – at least I had a fighting chance of walking away. Maybe.

'No weapons,' Jake announced loudly, 'and no holds barred.' He raised his hand in the air, looked around at the crowd like a gladiator match, and shouted, 'Kill him!'

As soon as Jake was out of the way, Zeke came forward. He was crouching like a wrestler and leering at me, his long hair hanging loose. I also noticed he had twin rings in his left earlobe and rings on most fingers. The finger rings would cause a problem, being a substitute knuckle duster, but the other ones I could use.

Pua hung back for now, no doubt sizing me up and assessing my capabilities.

'You gunna dance around all day, sweetheart?' I said to Zeke. 'Or you wanna get...'

I hadn't finished my sentence when he rushed me, arms out and going for the big tackle.

I couldn't have that.

I stepped out of the way, pushed his closest arm aside and came at him as he was turning. A snap kick to his thigh as a distraction, a handful of his long, greasy hair and I yanked his head back. I hooked my finger into one of his earrings and ripped it out. Blood sprang to the surface and he screeched with pain, but I wasn't finished with him yet. While he was distracted and grabbing at his ear and hair, I slammed an elbow into his throat, the point of my elbow impacting hard against his Adam's apple.

He gave a gasping wheeze, his eyes bugged, and Pua's huge frame filled my peripheral vision.

I stepped, twisted, yanking Zeke with me by the hair, and I got him between me and the big monster. The haymaker that Pua was throwing at me hit Zeke cleanly and smashed his eye socket.

Shoving the shrieking Zeke forward as a battering ram, I crashed into Pua and drove him back. He took a step back and stopped, and that was the end of the movement. Instead of Zeke knocking him over, the near-unconscious prospect became the meat in our sandwich. I jabbed past him, landing one on Pua's jaw.

He shook his head and threw one straight back, glancing off my temple hard enough to make me stagger.

The crowd cheered and urged him on. Pua pushed Zeke aside and came at me like a Terminator, a hard ball of aggression and hate. I danced away from him, sizing up my next move. His eyes were fixed on me and he kept coming, determined to rip me apart. I had no doubt that he could.

I backed up too far and got shoved from behind, sending me staggering forward, and Pua was on me in a flash. One hit to the chest, another to the side of the head and a third up into the ribs.

They were big, solid hits and they hurt and the rib shot sent a burst of sharp pain through my gut. I ducked away, spinning and getting past Pua as he came in with a big right-hander for my head. Had it connected, it would have knocked me flat, but instead it went over the top and left him exposed.

I got a good swing behind a left hook into his kidney, came back with a solid right to the ribs and then did it again. He took the hits with a grunt, turned and threw a massive left at my face. I moved too slow and it knocked me off my feet.

I went down, rolled and came up just in time to take a boot to the guts which lifted me off my feet and sent me to my knees again. Unable to breathe, I stayed where I was, bracing myself for the next hit. It was a head shot this time, a kick that exploded a rainbow of colours across my vision and bowled me like a ten-pin. I scrambled as best I could while still trying to breathe, getting away from Pua to give myself time.

It's never a good fight when you're not the one landing the hits and so far I'd barely fired a shot.

That needed to change, and fast.

54

The truck slowed as they entered the back street that gave access to the school. Gemma reasoned that going in the back was probably the safest route, and as she pulled up at the dead-end of the long street, she couldn't see anyone around. She turned the truck around and switched it off.

As soon as she got out she could hear them – motorbikes revving and men cheering and yahooing. It sounded like it was coming from within the school itself.

'Wait here, Aroha,' she told their passenger, and Aroha nodded painfully.

She'd been knocked around by the fast driving, but she didn't want to complain. She knew they had a job to do and she wouldn't slow them up.

Gemma checked the Rossi again, patted her pockets and pouches, and looked to Alex.

'Good to go?'

He nodded, trying to hide his nervousness. 'Yep.'

'Let's go.'

THE BRONZE-COLOURED PATROL rolled into town, nice and easy, nobody aware of its approach until it was already there.

Some of the escaped prisoners had gone walkabout and others were up at the hall and the school. A bunch of them were lounging on an empty section on the main drag, backing onto scrubland that led down to the highway. Smokes and bottles were being passed around and several of them were either asleep or passed out. A couple of patched Bandits were hanging with them, talking shit.

Further up the road, Guppy and his boys were walking down, making no effort to hide.

The wagon eased to a stop and the four operators debussed quickly, weapons at the ready.

The escapees and their Bandit mates were on their feet fast, startled by the sudden appearance, but not fast enough. They found themselves covered by four assault rifles, brandished by four mean-looking dudes in camo kit.

'Who's your head honcho?' Mickey said, directing the question towards the two Bandits.

'Who the fuck're you?' one of them sneered. 'Who the fuck's askin', homo?'

'I'm asking,' Mickey growled. 'Are you fuckin' deaf?'

The Bandit stepped up, puffing his chest out and eyeballing him. He was a big unit. There was a blur of movement and Mickey kicked him in the balls, swept his legs and dumped him in a heap on the ground.

He scanned the group. Nobody else moved. The Bandit on the ground vomited and cupped his squashed plums.

'Next please,' Mickey said.

Nobody even twitched. It was clear these guys weren't here to win hearts and minds. He looked down at the groaning Bandit on the ground.

'That's for beating up that old lady, you useless piece of shit,' he said. 'Count yourself lucky I don't put a fuckin' hole in your head and do us all a favour.'

He turned back to the other Bandit, who was watching silently. He was older and smaller than the first guy.

'You,' Mickey said. 'Who's your head honcho, and where is he?'

The guy gave a shrug.

'Dunno, cuz.'

'Well, fuck me.' Mickey glanced at Turk, who was covering to his left. 'Are they all this smart?'

'Gunna be a long day,' Turk said, his eyes never leaving the criminals before him. 'Unless we go to Plan B.'

Mickey grinned. 'Yeah, we could do Plan B.'

The Bandit swallowed and flicked his gaze between the two of them. The other gangster was still rolling on the ground and moaning.

'What's Plan B?' the Bandit asked.

Mickey shrugged. 'Usually, we just start shooting people.'

PUA WASN'T PREPARED to give an inch.

He came in fast, both fists jabbing at me to keep me on the move. I blocked one and it was like being hit by a car. My forearm went numb and I was forced into a backwards scramble again to get space. He went for a big hook and I ducked it, pushed the arm upwards with both hands, and came in with my best right hook to his ribs.

It was a hook that had knocked men down before, but it hardly seemed to register on his radar.

Pua absorbed it, turned, and smashed me square on the forehead with a big left jab.

I hit the deck on my back, tumbled head over heels and ended up on my knees with him bearing down on me. He wasn't grinning or laughing, just fixated on me and getting the job done. The Bandits in the background were whooping, sensing blood. This was it – all over in seconds. If I didn't get up now, I was fucked.

As Pua closed in, his huge fists clenched, I came up. A hint of a smile crossed his face until the handful of dirt and grit filled his eyes and mouth. He slapped at his face and I crash-tackled him, no arms, just a hard shoulder straight in the gut. I drove with my legs, pushing him backwards, and threw a leg behind his.

He tripped, stumbled and went down on his back, roaring like a wounded beast. I stayed on my feet and landed a fast kick between his legs. He groaned and grabbed for his crushed balls, and the crowd let me know what they thought. Pua was trying to get up when Zeke came back at me, unsteady on his feet but game enough to have a go. His face was blotchy red and purple and he was wheezing loudly.

I slapped his grabbing hands away and opened up the blade of the pocket knife in the commotion. Zeke was open and I punched him hard in the throat, driving the blade straight in like a lance.

His eyes bugged and he clutched at his windpipe as he dropped to his knees, blood flowing freely through his fingers. I let him go and turned back to the bigger threat, tucking the knife back into my pocket with the blade still open. It gave me more confidence that it was now one down, one to go. It didn't help that the one to go was a friggin' monster.

Pua had got his feet under him with one hand on the ground, and was looking for me. His eyes locked on and I could see the hatred there. He started to move and I knew it was now or never. I rushed him, side stepping at the last second as he came towards me in a low tackle. He got hold of my T-shirt as we passed and he yanked hard, pulling me off-balance.

My right boot got him in the back of the knee, buckling it and making him stumble, then it came again, a side kick this time. His right knee folded outwards at an ugly angle and he roared in pain, collapsing away from me. He let go of my T-shirt and went down.

Before he hit the deck I was over the top from behind, jerking his patch forward over his head then backwards so it covered his face. He grabbed at my hands and I slammed a knee into his spine, pulling him back into it then hitting it again. He got both hands onto my forearms and gripped, digging his fingers in. I could feel his sharp nails cutting in.

I locked on with the patch vest, levering him back against my knee as I put all my effort into suffocating him with his own patch.

Pua was a big strong man but the feeling of suffocating brought any man down to size, and I knew he would have an overwhelming sense of panic and just needing to be free. He ripped at my arms and bucked against me but I hung on for grim death – preferably his, not mine. It seemed to take forever before his struggling weakened but I knew I had him on the ropes when he let go of my arms and tried to pull the vest away from his face instead.

The Bandits were screaming manically, threats and abuse for me and encouragement for my opponent, but it didn't matter. Pua's hands dropped to his sides, flapping feebly for a minute before going limp. He stopped moving and just slumped back on his heels.

I stayed where I was, making sure the fucker wasn't faking, until my arms ached so much I had to let go. The body flopped to the side and lay still. I stood over him, breathing hard, and looked for Jake. We locked eyes as he came into the circle, moving cautiously. If he was surprised by the outcome, he gave no sign of it.

I broke his stare to scan the rest of the Bandits. They had gone silent and were waiting, unsure what to do. Waiting for a sign from their leader.

Jake drew the Sig from his belt and pointed it at me.

I guessed that was their sign.

THEY CLIMBED onto the roof of the closest building, which was maybe a classroom or an arts room, Gemma boosting Alex up first so he could pull her up. The roof was sloped and they made their way to the apex, lying flat and peering over the top. They had an excellent view of the school grounds, and it was immediately apparent that had arrived just in the nick of time.

A ring of vehicles and thugs formed a makeshift colosseum where

Mark was fighting with two guys, the surrounding gangsters cheering and whooping.

It was obvious that Mark was quite literally fighting for his life.

Gemma sighted in with her husband's rifle, settling the crosshairs of the scope on the Bandit standing in the bed of the ute. He was carrying some kind of assault rifle and looking around, but half the time he was looking at the fight going on behind him.

She shifted her gaze slightly to check the progress of the fight.

One guy was down on the ground and Mark was grappling with a huge man. It looked like he was trying to choke the guy with his own vest.

She shifted her aim back to the lookout.

'What d'you think?' she whispered.

'Looks like Mark's winning,' Alex whispered back. 'But what happens after that?'

He watched through the binoculars, and gave a gasp. 'I think he just killed that guy.'

Gemma nodded to herself. She'd seen it for herself. The big man was down and Mark had his hands on his hips, his shoulders heaving. She knew in her heart that the other man was dead, and it made her gut churn.

She saw another gangster step forward from the circle. The guard on the ute turned to see. The man facing Mark raised a pistol.

'Oh Jesus,' she whispered, and shifted her aim to the man with the pistol.

They were a good hundred metres away and she didn't know if she could hit him from there, even with the scope.

But she didn't want to see her husband murdered before her eyes.

THE BLACK EYE of the pistol weaved slightly in Jake's grip, but it never drifted from my face. There was no way he could miss at this range.

'Deal's a deal,' I rasped, my voice thick with the exertion of the fight. 'Two on one...winner walks away.'

Jake turned his head and spat, his eyes never leaving me.

'Don't you know?' he said. 'Never trust a criminal.'

I sucked down another breath, my heart jackhammering in my chest.

'Thought you're a man of your word,' I said, lying through my teeth. 'Not some cheap hood rat.'

Jake's face tightened and the Sig barrel trembled.

'Like I said…'

And that's when the shooting started.

Two shots at first, one louder than the other, and heads turned. I recognised the .357 Magnum crack and the lighter pop of a 9mm, and knew help had arrived. The Bandits froze, nobody knowing where the shots had come from, then more shots came and I heard a yell.

With Jake distracted, I took my chance. I crash-tackled him in the ribs and knocked him off his feet, wrenching the Sig from his hand as soon as he was down. He shouted a warning to his buddies but I was already moving. I stepped over him, firing a shot down into him as I moved, and I ran for the nearest vehicle.

The gangsters were starting to scatter now, some firing wildly in different directions, and one of them turned towards me with a shotgun in his hands. I fired three fast shots and he dropped then I was past him, getting in behind a car and ducking down. The Bandits were all yelling and shooting and the din was overwhelming. I had to get out of there but with bullets flying in all directions it would be madness to run just yet.

Peering around the car, I tried to figure out where the cavalry was.

55

The first shots had thrown the gang into disarray and Gemma was pretty sure she hadn't even hit anyone yet.

She levered another round into the chamber and scanned the scene through the scope. Most of the Bandits had taken cover behind the vehicles, but one guy was just standing out in the open with an assault rifle in his hands, firing bursts at one of the classrooms over to her right.

She sighted in on his chest and fired, and felt a buzz when he staggered back then fell on his butt. He tried to get up and one of his buddies ran forward to get him, but the wounded man accidentally fired and knocked his mate over. She could hear screaming and the second guy was thrashing on the ground. The man she'd shot flopped down and lay still.

Beside her, Alex was firing at the closest vehicle, where she could see at least a couple of gangsters hiding. One of them popped up and fired towards them, bullets whistling overhead. Alex returned fire and the guy ducked back, then the second one sent a couple of shots their way, ricocheting off the roof below them.

'Gas tank,' Gemma muttered. 'Hit the gas tank.'

She could see where the fuel cap was on her side of the vehicle, and she sighted on it. While Alex traded shots with the two guys and chaos reigned, she fired shot after shot at the gas tank area. Finally she saw fuel spurting out onto the ground and shifted her aim, getting another hole in the tank.

She couldn't see Mark, but as she sighted in again with her last round, she hoped like hell he was behind cover. She squeezed the trigger, the Rossi nudged into her shoulder, and the car exploded in a ball of flame.

Gemma ducked back down, feeling the heat of the flames and hearing impacts as pieces of the car smacked into the building. Windows shattered from the shockwave.

Screams sounded and she tried to block them out as her trembling fingers fed fresh rounds into the tube of the Rossi.

She worked the lever and came back on line again, scanning below. One gangster lay flat several metres from the burning wreck, his body in flames. She couldn't see the other guy.

BLACK SMOKE WAS POURING UPWARDS from the car that had exploded and the heat was intense, even from where I was. If nothing else, it had thrown the Bandits into more panic, which would hopefully be to my advantage.

I had spotted the two heads on the roofline, trading shots with the Bandits, and hoped there was more of them somewhere.

I was working out how best to get to them when a fat Bandit came scurrying up from another vehicle and squatted down beside me, wheezing. He had a Steyr in his hands and was sweating like a pig.

'Where is he, bro?' he panted.

I looked at him for a moment before realising he had mistaken me for a Bandit. He clocked his mistake at the same time and reeled back, trying to bring his weapon around, but a pistol was always going to be faster than a rifle at close range.

I shot him twice in the chest and he flopped down without a sound. Snatching the rifle from his hands, I shoved the Sig into my waistband and ran for the closest building. It was a clear fifty metres and I took a deep breath and went for it.

I'd barely gone two steps before a hog roared behind me and I heard a shout. I spun, dropping to a knee and opened fire on the bikie bearing down on me. He spilled off and tumbled and I dived out of the way as the Harley careened past me.

I got up and ran again, hearing more shouts behind me, then shots cracking the air nearby. I ducked and weaved, trying to make myself as hard a target as possible, barely even breathing as I went for gold.

The classroom I was going to was getting peppered with bullets, windows blowing out and bullets punching holes in the fibrolite panels. I jinked one last time and got round the side, finally taking a breath, but bullets were still punching through the thin walls and coming out my side.

The building where my rescuers were was another twenty or so metres away, and I could see them on the roofline, still firing back towards the Bandits. The thump of rounds was both exhilarating and scary, and I could see the building they were on was taking heavy hits. It wouldn't be long before they were blown off the roof by the overwhelming numbers of gangsters.

Looking closer, I recognised Gemma's head behind a scoped rifle which sounded very much like my Rossi. I smiled to myself, edged to the far corner of the building, and took a kneeling position. Leaning around the corner, I could see a pair of Harleys moving up the far side of the field, trying to outflank them.

The Steyr had a basic 3x scope and I settled it on the nearest rider. The second burst I fired nailed him and he fell straight off, the second guy accelerating past him. I tracked him for a few seconds before getting a burst onto his machine. It wobbled but didn't go down, and it took several more rounds to drop him.

Rounds started coming my way again and I ducked back to the other corner, dropping out the magazine to check my ammo supply. Four rounds left, plus the Sig. It wasn't looking good.

I heard my name being shouted and turned to see that Alex had come down off the roof and was waving at me from cover, pointing towards the road over behind them. I got the message and gave him a big thumbs-up.

He waved back excitedly, pointing and shouting. By the time I realised what he was on about, the two Bandits sprinting forward were almost on me. One had a baseball bat in his hands that he swung at me with all his might as soon as he got close enough. I ducked and dropped, shoving the Steyr up to try and protect my head.

It was knocked out of my hand and I tumbled to the ground awkwardly, the bat man staggering past me with his own momentum. The other guy was carrying an M4 – my M4 – and fired a shot past me as I got my knees and yanked the Sig from my waistband. I fired from the hip and dropped him with three rounds, twisting to see the bat man coming at me again, the wooden bat raised above his head for a downward strike. I punched out and put a round in his gut.

He stumbled forward, the bat dropping as he lurched and fell beside me. I ignored him and went to the other guy, snatching up the M4. He had my gun belt on and I took a few seconds to recover it, buckle it, and check the mag on the Bushmaster. Nearly full.

Checking round the corner, I could see the Bandits hadn't advanced any further, but were still firing sporadically towards the roof where their targets had been.

Gemma had joined Alex and they were waving me forward. I shoved the Sig in my belt – it seemed ridiculous to carry three pistols, but I wasn't leaving weapons behind me – slung the M4 across body in my right hand and grabbed up the Steyr in my left.

I sprinted at an angle, keeping the classroom between me and the enemy for as long as possible before cutting across towards them and drawing fire.

It was well wide and didn't stop me from tagging in behind them as they raced back towards the road. I saw our Nissan parked there, nobody in sight. Gemma made to throw me the keys when we got to it, but I could hear hogs coming.

'You drive,' I said. 'Alex in the front and me in the back.'

I leaped in the tray and settled myself against the rear of the cab as the truck took off with squealing tyres. We got to the end of the road and Gemma threw a hard left, joining the main drag that headed through the town centre. The thunder of four hogs roaring up behind us was deafening. I got the Bushmaster up and started firing, snapping two-shot semi-auto bursts at them.

One of the bikes swerved and wobbled, the rider overbalanced and the bike tipped, skidding along the road on its side in a shower of sparks. The other three carried on chasing and I tried to keep my aim steady as the truck bumped and jarred at speed. I was managing to keep them back, but it would take more than that to stop them.

The town centre was coming up fast and I knew there was a series of speed bumps there. At this rate we would wipe out if Gemma didn't hit the picks.

She took a right turn too fast and I felt the rear wheels sliding beneath me. I grabbed the side for support as the tail slid out. I could hear swearing from the cab behind me as she fought the wheel.

The three bikes closed up and I saw one of them had moved a rifle forward on its sling under his arm, gripping it and getting ready to fire.

The truck straightened up and I braced myself again, getting the M4 back in the shoulder. I pumped several shots at the pursuing bikers, making them separate and slow, then focussed on the guy with the rifle. He returned fire but I figured he'd be doing well to get anywhere near me.

I steadied my aim as best I could and squeezed off a last double-tap before the mag ran dry. My last round struck the gunman's machine and I saw petrol spraying into the slipstream from the tank in front of him. He was getting soaked and his buddies behind him cut wider to stay out of the spray.

I dropped the empty magazine out and slapped a new one in, released the bolt and was good to go again. My first round hit him in the arm and he fired a shot of his own. Whether it was that or my second shot that caused the explosion, I didn't know.

Either way, the result was brutally spectacular. The gas fumes ignited and the bike erupted in a flash of fire. The rider caught alight and screamed in terror, the bike still roaring forward as it became engulfed in a fireball. Gemma must have seen it in her rear-view mirror because she accelerated hard to get away from the burning bike.

The bike exploded in a fiery blast, shrapnel whizzing everywhere.

I covered my head and ducked down as bits of shrapnel pinged off the bodywork of the truck.

One of the other bikers was hit by shrapnel and he swerved off the road, hit the kerb at somewhere around the ton, and became airborne. The hog flew through the air with the rider desperately hanging on, over a front yard and crashed into the roof of a small white church. The rider was catapulted over the handlebars and was still airborne when we took a hard left and I lost sight of him.

'Motherfucker,' I breathed, getting myself set again and scanning for threats.

There was none. The burning hog was pouring smoke into the sky, and the last remaining bikie had stopped back at the junction, watching us as we escaped.

I fired a last couple of rounds in his direction and grinned when I saw him duck. I threw him the bird and leaned back against the cab, sucking down breaths. My body was battered but the elation I felt overrode the pain.

I couldn't quite believe we had pulled it off, although we weren't out of the woods just yet. We barrelled along the country roads and were in Pokeno in no time. For years it had been a two-horse town where motorists stopped at the famous ice cream shop when driving between Auckland and Hamilton. There had been little else there until developers took hold and the housing exploded.

A Chinese dairy factory had set up shop and various other businesses followed, but it was still tiny. We raced through it and didn't slow until we'd got through town and reached the on ramp to join the highway.

We pulled to the side and Gemma got out, leaving the engine running. Gemma being Gemma, she had even indicated when she pulled over. I climbed down and she grabbed me in a hug tight enough to make me gasp.

'Don't you ever do that again,' she said, her voice muffled in my neck.

I squeezed her back and told her I wouldn't, then she told me I had to drive because she was shaking too much. It was true – the emotion and adrenaline were easing off and she was trembling.

I took the keys, she jumped in the back with Aroha – I hadn't realised she was there until I got behind the wheel – and I gassed it. There was still the chance that the Bandits would give chase, and I didn't want to hang around.

BLASTING NORTH UP THE HIGHWAY, Mickey spotted a black Nissan truck heading the other way.

He clocked a couple of blokes and a couple of women in it, with at least a couple of longs between them. The guy driving was the prisoner they'd seen earlier back in Meremere.

'Interesting,' he muttered.

'Wanna stop them, Mick?' Turk called out over the roar of the engine and the wind buffeting them through the open windows.

Mickey shook his head. 'Keep going. I wanna find these shitheads.' He shot a grin at his driver. 'The Smash are coming to town, motherfuckers. Brace yourselves.'

WE MADE it to Mercer in record time and diverted to the place where I had stashed the quad bike. I swapped onto that and Alex took over driving the ute, and I followed them through Mercer and out into the open country. After all the action and adrenaline and fear, it felt good to be on the quad again with the wind in my face. Even though my body ached all over, I was buzzing from the gunfight. Nothing had ever given me such a high, and I understood now why soldiers got addicted to the action. It was terrifyingly dangerous but exhilarating in equal measure.

I pushed my thoughts to one side and focussed on following the truck in front of me. It would lead me home and home was where I needed to be.

END

The **Early Warning** series continues...

BONUS CHAPTER

THE DIVISION SERIES #1

SMOKE AND MIRRORS

Baghdad, Iraq
Two years ago

It wasn't called the Highway to Hell for nothing.

Driving on the highway from the city to Baghdad International Airport was like 200 miles of dodgems, only every dodgem potentially carried a bomb or a carload of ruthless bastards who wanted to slice off your head on Al-Jazheera and drag your corpse through the streets.

Archer loved it and loathed it at the same time; the thrill of the risk was intoxicating, but the reality of it going bad was too terrifying to contemplate. In his team of PMCs they had a deal-last man standing finished any wounded then took one himself.

Deny the pricks the pleasure of doing it themselves.

His team, he thought to himself. For about another hour, they were still his team. After that he was on a big bird to LA to meet up with a tidy American Army Major, to spend 3 weeks eating, drinking and screwing, in no particular order. After 3 weeks R&R he was coming back, and they'd be his team again.

He cast a lazy eye to the driver on his right, big Grunter, a bald former SWAT team officer in Johannesburg. He was built like a house and ate constantly when he wasn't working out. He had seen more action in Jo'burg than most squaddies in Iraq. He drove the Nissan Patrol like it was a Tonka toy.

Behind Grunter sat Jacko, a former Para sergeant who had served a full 20 years and gone straight into the private sector to earn his pension. The Brit was a tattooed chain smoker and notorious practical-joker. Archer's boxers still scratched from when Jacko had drowned them in starch and turned them to cardboard.

In the rear of the wagon was the gunner, on this occasion Bula, the Fijian alcoholic who had served with 22 SAS for a decade before going private. Constantly smiling and hung over he was nearly fifty and the veteran of a dozen wars around the globe.

Archer kept his eyes moving, scanning his arc to the left, the barrel of his Russian AK-47 resting on his left knee, finger alongside the trigger guard, stock folded for ease of movement. Vehicles all around them, moving like people on a conveyer belt, an endless stream towards the airport and its surrounds. Iraqis stared back at the white faces with either indifference or open disdain and hostility. Not fear. These people were not afraid of the heavily armed men in the packet, identical in their polo shirts and wrap around shades. Men like this had come and gone, and would always do so, and it meant nothing. They meant nothing; just another white face.

The sun was at a dangerous angle, and Grunter was squinting behind his shades and the sun visor. The white Renault in front of them carried their other team members and their clients, a pair of oil company execs who had spent a week schmoozing and were on their way home. Archer was accompanying them, which suited the team because they could tie in the drop-off with picking up a new team member on his way in from the UK. Dusty, up front with his fellow former Royal Marine, Tim, would be running the team in Archer's absence. He was a good man but probably a little more conservative than Archer would have liked. Although conservative wasn't always a bad thing in this part of the world.

Dusty was giving the constant commentary that they could hear over their earpieces, identifying any risks or potential trouble spots as they came into range.

'White truck, right, 150. Man in back with AK. 100 now, not aware. Closing up, still not aware...'

Bula's voice came over the radio then.

'Hey, red Beamer coming from behind, left of us, 3 or 4 boys. Unfriendlies, keeping eyes.'

Archer caught sight in the wing mirror of the BMW coming up on the left, two boys in the front and at least another in the back. All of them had eyes on the Patrol, and he could see the tension in their bodies.

At the same time, Dusty came back on.

'Dead dog, right, 100.'

IED, thought Archer, thumbing off his safety catch at the same time.

'Drop back Grunter,' he ordered and felt the Patrol slow immediately, 'eyes up guys. I've got the left, keep your arcs.'

The red BMW was almost even with them now and he could see two in the back now. The angle was no good for seeing weapons though. He rested his finger lightly on the trigger and kept one eye on the car and one on the rest of the surrounds. The gap between the Patrol and the Renault had opened up slightly, allowing them more room to move in an IA.

Archer saw a flicker of movement from the back seat as the closest passenger lifted the barrel of an AK into view. All eyes from the car were on his now in his wing mirror and he knew it was game on.

'Grunter, hit it!' he barked, the AK coming into view properly as the window came down. He raised his own AK as Grunter jerked the wheel left and smashed into the front wing of the Beamer.

Archer triggered a burst through the window straight into the interior of the car as it lurched to the left, at the same time as an almighty explosion erupted from the right, strong enough to rock the Patrol and blow out windows in the cars around it. The windscreen shattered under the force of debris and Archer felt stings across his face and arm.

Traffic closed up all around them as cars crashed into each other, and Grunter jerked the wheel left again, smashing into a beaten up pick up that had drifted in front of him. He gunned the big engine and shoved the pick up out of the way, clearing a space to get to the shoulder of the road. The white Renault was also moving left, seeking a way clear of the carnage.

Archer saw the BMW coming back, accelerating up on the left, openly displaying AKs out the windows now.

'Contact left! Contact left!' he barked into his mouthpiece, one hand depressing the pressel switch on his chest and the other levelling the AK. He cut loose another burst, longer this time, raking the windscreen of the BMW to blind the driver. Jacko had slid across the backseat and opened up too, a long burst into the back which took out the closest passenger.

Too late, he realised they had made the wrong move, both vehicles coming to the left.

A second explosion detonated on the shoulder of the road, bigger than the first and almost directly in front of the Renault. The front of the car lifted off the ground in a shower of dust and dirt and flame, crashing back down at an angle and almost rolling, rocking on its springs as it settled back down again at the edge of a smoking crater.

Grunter was blinded and ran straight into the back of the Renault, shunting it forward before he managed to stop.

Surrounded by a dust cloud and with screams in his ears, Archer shouted, 'Debus, debus! IA!'

He threw the door open and leaped out, snapping open the butt stock of the AK and shouldering it, seeking targets.

The boys in the BMW knew they were there and would be using the Patrol as a start point, so they needed to get clear quickly, secure the guys from the Renault, and move.

Archer moved forward as per their IA drills, bellowing, 'Moving!' and making a magazine change on the run.

He got to the wreck of the Renault and wrenched open the left rear door. He could see immediately that the two execs were shaken and scratched but okay. Dusty was bleeding in the front passenger's seat, the front of his armour saturated from a wound in his face. Tim was dead, most of his head gone and sprayed across the execs in the back.

Archer seized the closest client by the arm and yanked him out, shouting, 'Move! Move now!'

Gunfire sounded behind him above the heavy buzz in his ears but he ignored it, focussing on the task at hand. The exec tumbled out and Archer pushed him to the ground a couple of metres away with an order to stay down. The second one was frozen and wouldn't budge. Archer grabbed him by the collar and jerked him across the back seat but he locked his arms and legs against the door frame and began wailing like a scared child.

Not breaking stride, Archer thumped him in the face with a left jab and stunned him, then yanked him out and pushed him down beside his mate. Kneeling over them he scanned around, seeing the BMW pulled up near the Patrol, all doors open and fire coming from behind it. Jacko and Grunter were deployed at each end of the Patrol, trading shots with the Beamer boys. Bula was cutting around another vehicle, the RPK in his hands looking like a .22 to a normal sized man. He was seeking an angle to out flank the enemy.

Archer slapped both execs on the head and shouted at them to stay down, then pushed up and returned to the Renault. The front passenger door was buckled and wouldn't open. He used his rifle barrel to clear the broken glass and reached in to Dusty. The former Marine was barely conscious, bleeding heavily from a nasty gouge to his left cheek and another slice across his forehead. His nose looked broken, and Archer realised he had probably smashed his face into the dash. A quick check revealed no other obvious injuries.

'Come on you whinging fucken Pom!'

Archer slung his AK and grabbed his mate under the arms, heaving him up and dragging him through the window. He dragged him across to the execs and lay him down. Ripping Dusty's own field dressing from his webbing Archer pressed it against the cheek wound and used his arm to wipe some of the blood away. He ripped a length of duct tape from his own webbing and secured it across the dressing and half way round Dusty's head.

He checked the lads again and saw Bula had got distracted. Somebody had opened up from the far side of the road at him, and he had now taken a knee behind a vehicle and was trying to pick off the target through the wreckage around him.

Archer moved right, keeping well clear of his own lads' arcs, AK in the shoulder. He could see two of the Beamer boys behind the engine block, each with an AK, taking turns to rise and pop a short burst at Jacko and Grunter.

Archer dropped flat on his belly and took aim. He could see the side of one of the boys around the edge of the wrecked BMW, and let loose a quick double tap. A scream sounded and the gunman fell backwards into full view. Archer gave him a longer burst that shook him like a bad disco dancer and he dropped his AK, writhing in the dirt. His mate wasn't stupid though and kept his position behind the engine block, his feet hidden by the wheel.

Archer saw his gun barrel poke up above the bonnet of the BMW and readied himself. The gun edged up horizontally and loosed off a spray of rounds blindly, the bullets sweeping across the side of the Patrol and punching more holes in it.

Jacko was closest to Archer and returned a burst of his own, before yelling, 'Stoppage!'

Archer saw him ripping his magazine off and slapping in a new one, then yanking at the bolt.

'Stoppage!' he shouted again, indicating a jam.

The other Beamer boy obviously understood some English because he saw his opportunity to seal the deal. Archer rose at the same time as the insurgent and double tapped him in the chest. The Iraqi fell back behind the car, his AK firing wildly into the sky.

'Moving!'

Archer moved forward and right, seeing the three Iraqis behind the car. One dead on his back, the second rolling on his side with the AK still in his hand, trying to bring it round, the third at the back trading shots with Grunter.

He put a burst into the wounded gunman, the third oblivious to his presence, and moved in closer. The third gunman saw him now and swung round to meet the new threat, but too late. As he moved, Grunter took his head off at the shoulders with a triple burst, and Archer caught him in the front as he went down.

Archer put another burst into the head of the first man, and repeated it on the second. Grunter had moved forward now and finished off what was left of his own target.

More gunfire sounded from the roadway, a couple of single AK shots then a sustained burst of machine gun fire.

Bula came back through the dust at a jog, the RPK in his hands and blood dribbling from his leg. He was still grinning.

'Got 'im bro,' he shouted, taking a knee near Jacko, covering arcs again.

'Grunter, get the wagon going,' Archer ordered, 'Jacko with me. Bula; with Grunter.'

They moved quickly, Jacko covering the growing crowd of onlookers as Archer got to the execs and Dusty.

He took a knee over them and covered an arc, hearing horn blasts and roaring Humvee engines as an American PMC team approached from the rear. There were smashing sounds as the column forced its way through the traffic, even though it would have been easier to go wide into the desert.

Not much difference between some of the PMCs and their service comrades, Archer thought.

Grunter got the Patrol going and manoeuvred fully onto the shoulder, Bula trotting behind him as he made his way forward. They quickly loaded the execs into the backseat and onto the floor, Jacko over them.

Archer got Dusty into the back as well then moved back to the Renault. Bula got a Union Jack out and slung it across the back of the Patrol to face the Yanks when they arrived. The last thing they wanted now was friendly fire.

Tim's legs were stuck under the steering wheel and Archer was working at freeing them, trying to ignore the sticky mess around him, when he heard the Yank packet arrive. He got the right leg free and got Tim half out the window when he heard a burst of fire.

Cradling Tim in his arms he threw a glance over his shoulder, instinct telling him this was going bad.

A Humvee was pulled up near the Patrol, and a gunner was leaning out the window with his M4, shouting at Bula who stood near the back of the Patrol with his RPK.

'Oh shit...'

Archer let Tim down and started to move back to his team, waving and shouting at the soldier, but it was too late.

The gunner was obviously amped up and used to giving orders that were obeyed. Bula was also amped up but still in control, but that wasn't the problem. He was holding a machine gun and had dark skin, and even though Archer clearly understood he was shouting 'Security patrol! We're on your side!' the young Yank obviously couldn't understand a Fijian accent.

The M4 burst off rounds and Bula went down.

'Fuck!'

Archer sprinted forward now, hands in the air, shouting, 'Cease fire! Cease fire!'

He got to the roadway and the Humvee emptied out. The gunslinger who had shot Bula darted towards him with his carbine raised, ready to finish him, convinced he had taken a Taleban down.

'Stand down you fucken moron!' Jacko bellowed at him, debussing with Grunter, both of them wise enough to leave their AKs behind.

The gunner swung his rifle towards them then paused as the two white men confronted him. His gaze went back to where Bula lay still in the dust.

'What the hell...'

He never finished his sentence because Grunter seized him by the throat with one big mitt and stripped him of his weapon with the other. He lifted the other guy onto his tip-toes and tossed the carbine aside.

Jacko went to Bula and Archer reached them just as the vehicle commander, a young surfer looking dude, pointed a rifle at Grunter's head.

'Stand down, boy,' he drawled, calm and quiet. 'Do it now.'

Grunter tossed the gunner aside like a rag doll and stepped back, hands raised and his face as impassive as ever. Jacko stood and came over. He had blood on his hands and rage in his eyes.

'He's dead,' he said flatly. He raised his hands to shoulder height, showing the blood on his hands to the Americans.

Archer sucked in a breath through his nose and felt grit in his eyes. The American squad were facing them, guns raised. Compared to his own team, these guys were the stereotypical private contractors in a company uniform of desert boots, sand khakis and navy blue polos, all with fingerless gloves, baseball caps and wrap around shades. Their armour vests were loaded with radios, spare mags and bulging pouches.

Archer recognised them straight away as Black Star operators. Known on the circuit as Death Star due to the high number of lives they both lost and took, they had a terrible reputation for questionable contacts. A couple of their guys were awaiting trial for wiping out an unarmed family in Fallujah the previous year. They were the last guys he wanted to tangle with when everyone was already hot under the collar.

He knew for a fact that many of their guys were either shell shocked vets who should never have been trusted with a gun again, or former soldiers who had been dishonourably discharged. Drug use was apparently rife among their ranks and allegations of looting had been made.

'We're private security,' he told the team leader, 'we've got clients on board and got hit by a couple of IEDs. We've got one KIA and a casualty on board; we could do with a medic.'

His gaze shifted to the gunner who'd shot Bula, standing aside rubbing his throat and eyeing Grunter resentfully.

'Now we've got two KIAs, thanks to you.'

'Ahh thought he's a Taleban,' the guy whined to his commander. 'All them rag heads look the same, sarge.'

'He's Fijian, you fucken Dixie inbreed,' Jacko growled, his nostrils flaring.

The gunner also flared, and stepped forward.

'Who you callin' inbreed, boy?'

'Sergeant, call him off,' Archer warned, deliberately using the team leader's previous rank. He put a hand on Jacko's arm. 'Leave it Jacko.'

'Private!'

'I ain't no Dixie...'

They were nearly toe to toe now.

'Sergeant, control your man,' Archer said forcefully, taking a step forward.

Jacko's fist flashed out and flattened the young gunner's nose across his face, and Archer moved between them, pushing them both back. He turned, holding Jacko back, just in time to catch a jab from the gunner in the side of his face.

He shook it off, opened his mouth to speak again, and took another jab.

Enough's enough.

His own right uppercut came up full force and collected the Black Star gunman under his jaw, lifting him onto his toes and knocking him backwards with his eyes rolling back in his head.

A rifle butt smashed into the side of Archer's skull and everything went black.

MESSAGE FROM THE AUTHOR

Thanks for taking the time to read *Stand Fast*. I hope you enjoyed the third book in the **Early Warning** series. Join my mailing list on Facebook to hear about the release of the next book in the series...

I'd love it if you could please take the time to leave an online review of *Stand Fast* with your favourite book retailer.

If you'd like to know about new releases and receive a free book, sign up to my **Hitlist** on Facebook -

https://www.facebook.com/writer-angus-mclean

Cheers,
   Angus McLean

ACKNOWLEDGMENTS

The author would like to thank the advisers who have assisted with the writing of this book. They must remain anonymous for security reasons, but they (and only they) know who they are.

They are the true heroes who put their lives on the line to protect our freedoms. My sincerest gratitude goes out to them.

And once again, huge thanks to "Tori" who does my covers and provides great advice. You rock.

This is a work of fiction, and all errors are the responsibility of the author.

ABOUT THE AUTHOR

Angus McLean is a South Auckland Police officer.

His experience as a cop and a private investigator give his writing a touch of realism. He believes reading should be escapist entertainment and is inspired by the TV shows he watched as a youngster.

His real identity remains a secret.

www.writerangusmclean.com